I 1

INVISIBLE FUTURE

LINDSEY ANDERLE

Copyright

Printed in the United States of America

First Printing, October 2018

ISBN 978-0-692-19866-7

Book Cover Design by: www.ebooklaunch.com

You can find me on Facebook and Twitter –
Lindsey Anderle

Chapter One

I looked around my desk one last time, making sure everything was in its place before I left work for the night. I opened my briefcase to confirm that I had placed the manuscript I was currently editing in there. Working at Voodoo Publishing had its perks, such as getting off at three p.m. on Fridays.

I straightened the nameplate on my desk, feeling a warm glow of pride as I looked at the shine of 'Abigail Hendricks' for everyone to see. Satisfied that I had everything I needed, I hoisted the briefcase strap onto my shoulder and left the office area where I worked. There were six desks evenly spaced around the room, and I had the desk in the far back corner away from the door. Sometimes it felt like I was in my own little world because I wasn't close to most of the other editors in the room.

I headed to the elevator on the far side of the room, already looking forward to getting home. It had been a busy week, with new proposals showing up almost daily. I always felt bad for the potential books and authors that got turned down, but the truth was, some were just awful with their unedited manuscripts and clichéd plotlines.

I got into the elevator with two other people, all of us heading down and out. When the doors opened on the first floor, I said goodbye to them and walked out the front door. I turned right, heading for the parking garage. Getting into my car, I started the twenty-minute drive home. I lived in an apartment building with my best friend, Whitney Hamilton.

Reaching home, I went up the four flights to our apartment. I unlocked the door and saw Whitney was already there, cleaning up the living room, bass from the song she was listening to thumping loudly.

"Hey, Whitney!" I shouted over the music she had playing. I put my keys on the keyring and set my briefcase down.

"Abigail! Hey! I didn't hear you come in!" Whitney danced her way to the front hallway, pillow in her hand.

I rolled my eyes, smiling. With the music blaring, it was no surprise she hadn't heard me. I followed her to the living room.

Whitney went to the stereo and turned it down. "How was work?" she asked me.

"Oh, it wasn't too bad. I had to bring some work home with me to try to get some more done over the weekend," I answered, plopping down onto the couch.

Whitney tossed the pillow at me. "Not tonight, my friend! Tonight, you and I are going out. We are in sore need of a fun time."

I thought about resisting, knowing how much reading I had to get done. But seeing the pleading look on Whitney's face, I knew there was no point in trying.

I stood up. "Fine with me! I guess I better start getting ready then." Whitney was a bit of a bathroom hog, and I always had to beat her in there to ensure that I could get what I needed done.

By the time we were ready, we had gone back and forth between each other's closets a few times, mixing and matching our clothes, trying to find the right outfits to wear out. In the end, I settled on a green tank top and short black skirt with flats, while Whitney was in a hot pink dress with high heels.

Around eight p.m., we were walking the four blocks to our favorite bar, The Den. Being the beginning of the weekend, the streets were getting busy. Cars were constantly zooming by and people were filling up the sidewalks, making it feel cramped as we headed to our destination.

I looked down at Whitney's ridiculously tall heels. "I will never understand how you can walk in those." Her talent never ceased to amaze me.

Whitney grinned at me. "It's a gift. Besides, I have to weed out all of the short guys who don't meet my height requirement."

I laughed at that. Being only 5'5", I was pretty sure every man was taller than me, heels or no heels. Whitney was a few inches taller than I was and was also much stricter on her dating requirements.

We had reached the last intersection, waiting on the light to change. The Den was right across the street. Loud music was pouring out of the open door, and people were crowded around the entrance, waiting to go in. Others were standing around the outdoor seating, smoking cigarettes or chatting with their friends.

Two other men and a woman were waiting to cross as well. Finally, the light changed. We started to cross and neared the other side. I looked at Whitney, about to say something, when I heard tires squealing. A red four-door car was turning in front of us without slowing down at all and I felt the wind from it blow my skirt around, the sharp scent of burnt rubber stinging in my nose. I shrieked, frozen, until one of the men crossing with us grabbed my hand, pulling me over sharply.

I could hear screaming and crying. I was too shocked to really pay much attention to anything except the man beside me, still holding onto me. Fear had me frozen in place and clutching the man's hand tightly, unsure of where it was safe to move to.

The man who had grabbed my hand guided me to the sidewalk and peered down at me. "Are you okay?" he asked, looking me over for injuries. "That car almost ran you over!"

I just nodded, still dazed. Whitney ran over, tears staining her face. She hugged me tightly before examining me. "That car almost got you! Oh, my God! He didn't even stop or slow down! What if he had hit you, you could be dead!" she cried.

"I'm okay," I replied, finally coming back to myself. "Is everyone else okay?"

The man spoke up. "Everyone else is fine. The car sped off before anyone could get any info on it for the police." He looked disgusted at the thought of such a reckless driver like that staying on the road.

Whitney shook her head and carefully wiped at her face to make sure her makeup wasn't running. "Well, I guess we really need some drinks now!" She motioned to the man. "You and your friend are welcome to join."

I think she had finally noticed how attractive the man was. Being a little over six feet tall easily put him in her height bracket. He had chestnut brown hair and dark brown eyes. His dark blue plaid button-up shirt accentuated the muscles that I could tell were underneath. I knew if he turned around that I would be able to appreciate just how well his jeans fit him.

I was surprised when he turned and looked over at me and asked, "Is that all right with you?"

I blinked a couple of times before remembering to respond. Out of the corner of my eye, I could see Whitney reacting to the fact that the man was asking my opinion, a scowl on her face. I guess she had assumed he would be into her, since most men were.

"Um, yeah, that's fine with me," I managed to spit out. "I'm Abigail Hendricks and this is Whitney Hamilton."

The man held his hand out. "Lane Coleman. That there is my brother, Kent."

I shook Lane's hand and then his brother's. Kent looked pretty similar to Lane, but not quite as tall. I noticed dark brown eyes on him, too. He was wearing jeans and a button-down shirt as well, but my eyes kept drifting away from him to Lane. Kent just wasn't as impressive to me as his brother was.

Whitney clapped her hands once and gestured at the door to The Den. "Well, shall we?"

I could tell she was excited at the turn the night had taken. After the terrifying almost hit-and-run, of course. I followed her inside, slowing down to let my eyes adjust to the dimness inside. On the left wall was a bar running down the length of it, spotlights highlighting the different bottles of liquor. Throughout the floor were various tables and high tops, and on the right-hand wall were a handful of booths. Tonight, it was quite crowded, and we had to wait for a table. The bar was also full, with people pushing around each other to shout at the bartenders.

It felt like pure chaos from where I stood as a bystander. I couldn't imagine how the bartenders felt. Perfumes and colognes permeated the air around us, almost blocking out the smell of alcohol that seemed to be in every bar I've been in.

Someone came in the front door to my right, causing me to take a step back and bump into Lane. I quickly stepped away. "Oh, I'm sorry! I didn't realize you were right there."

Lane gave me a slow smile. "It's okay. It happens." He kept looking at me as if he were studying me.

After a minute, I realized I was staring at him, too. I cleared my throat and looked down before turning away from him. I widened my eyes at

Whitney, as if to ask for help. Luckily, she had always been good at reading my silent gestures.

"Oh, look, I see a table over there!" She pointed toward the middle of the room. Grabbing my hand, she started hauling me in that direction, Lane and Kent following us.

When we reached the table, Whitney turned to the two men. "If you'll excuse us for a moment, we'll be right back." She practically dragged me to the restroom, which was thankfully empty.

Turning to the mirror, Whitney started fluffing her hair. "This night started as a nightmare!"

I agreed with her, turning to examine myself in the mirror. My auburn hair was hanging flat, which seemed to always happen when I tried to curl it. My hazel eyes were framed by dark lashes that I had added mascara to. My cheeks were still red, probably more from my embarrassment over stepping into Lane than the blush I had applied. I reached into my pocket for my lip gloss, so I could at least have one thing that looked good.

Whitney finished with her hair and turned to me. "So, which one do you want? Me, personally, I kind of like Lane. He's got that tall, dark, and handsome thing going on."

My stomach flipped at that, though I wasn't sure why. I went into a bathroom stall to hide my reaction, not sure if it was broadcasted on my face.

"Yeah, I mean, whatever you want. They're both pretty cute." I rolled my eyes, knowing I was safe from view. Whitney tended to be extremely demanding when she set her eyes on something she wanted, disregarding anyone else's feelings on the matter.

Whitney banged on the stall door. "You done in there? They're not going to wait for us all night!"

I flushed the toilet, even though I hadn't used it. Opening the stall, I came out and saw Whitney by the door. She swung it open and left, with me following behind.

We got back to the table and Whitney immediately sat down next to Lane, who was across from Kent. I sat down slowly, not sure what to think anymore. I was actually kind of annoyed at Whitney for taking over and not really letting me have an opinion. *This is so typical of her*, I thought.

There were already four beers on the table, plus four shots of tequila. I saw Whitney glance at the beers with distaste. I knew she preferred mixed drinks and I wondered if she would drink them, because of Lane.

Lane passed out the shots, and then lifted his own. "To the four of us. To surviving the night." He looked at me as he said the toast, letting his smile slowly spread across his face. I noticed the corners of his eyes crinkling as he did this.

I blushed, feeling my face heat up. If I was to be honest with myself, Lane was the most handsome man I had ever met. But I wouldn't let myself think about it too much, for Whitney's sake.

We all raised up our glasses, clinked them together and drank. I winced, unused to drinking liquor. It burned as it ran down my throat. I pulled a beer over and drank, hoping to quench the burn. It helped a little bit.

Whitney had turned to Lane, engaging him in conversation, leaving me with Kent. I turned to him and saw him glancing around the room.

"So, have you been here before?" I asked.

"No, I haven't. My brother and I are new to the city, and tonight is the first chance we've had to really get out," Kent replied, turning in his chair to face me.

"Oh, really? Well, I'm glad you guys chose tonight to go out." I was thinking about almost getting hit by that car. If Lane and Kent had not been crossing the street with us, I didn't even want to think of what might have happened.

I glanced over at Lane and noticed him looking back at me. He gave a small smile and I ducked my head down, feeling embarrassed. I looked back at Kent. "So, what brought you guys here?"

Kent took a drink of his beer. "We both wanted something new. So, we moved to a completely new state, and gambled with the fact that we might run out of money before we find jobs." He looked at me, and it felt like he was trying to figure me out. "What do you do, Amy?"

I felt a flash of annoyance. Amy, really? Dumb guy couldn't even remember my name. "It's Abigail, actually," I said stiffly, and then heard a snort from across the table. I looked over and saw Lane trying to cover up the smile he couldn't quite hide. He was still paying attention to Whitney, but somehow, I knew he had been listening to us talk. "And I work at Voodoo Publishing as an editor."

Kent raised his eyebrows, looking impressed. "That's pretty cool. I hate reading, though."

I stared blankly at him. This could not be going any worse than it already was. I was starting to wish I had just stayed home and kept up with the pages that needed editing. Even horrible writing would have been better than talking to the man before me.

Lane chose that moment to stand up. "Another round for everyone?" he asked, pointing at us all. "Abigail, do you want to come and help me carry them?"

I was surprised but nodded yes. Glancing at Whitney, I could tell by the purse in her lips that she wasn't thrilled Lane had asked me instead of her.

We got up and walked to the bar, waiting our turn. Lane turned to me, studying my face. "So, how's your night going?"

I rolled my eyes. "Oh, great, you know. First, I almost *die*, and then I'm stuck talking to some guy who forgets my name." I felt my stomach drop, realizing who I was talking to. "Not that your brother's all bad, of course." I was trying to backtrack, and Lane knew it.

He chuckled, shaking his head. "Relax, Abby. I know you meant no harm."

I felt my face heat up at his nickname. Surprisingly, nobody called me by one. I was just Abigail and always had been.

"Actually," he continued, "I was kind of thinking that I wished I had been talking to you all night instead of..." He trailed off, his eyes drifting over to Whitney.

I followed his gaze, and saw Whitney watching us. Kent seemed to be trying to get her attention, waving his arms around, apparently describing something. I looked back at Lane. A lazy smile was on his face as he looked at me.

"What?" I asked, itching to reach up and feel my face or hair, sure that there must be something stuck in them.

He shook his head. "I've just never met anyone quite like you before." He stepped closer, causing me to catch my breath. "You interest me."

I let out a breathless laugh, stepping away from him and up to the bar. This was *not* happening. Guys like Lane just did not talk this way to me. "Easy there, tiger. We're just here to have some drinks. We happened to be at the same place at the same time."

Lane looked down at me, eyes roaming over my face. I felt like he could hear the doubt in my voice. It felt like it was oozing off my skin. "All right. Just drinks it is, then." He turned to the bartender and ordered four more beers and tequila shots.

Feeling awkward, I gathered up two shots and two beers, Lane taking the others. We wound our way back to our table where Whitney was obviously ignoring Kent, keeping her entire focus on us instead.

She turned as we approached. "Abigail, I need to use the restroom." She stared at me, her squinted, angry eyes trying to drill a message into my brain.

I nodded. "Um, yeah, so do I. We'll be right back." I looked at Lane, who was watching me as I walked by him. He lifted his hand and let it trail over mine as I passed him. My heart sped up and I froze for a second, shivering at the contact as I felt butterflies fluttering around in my stomach. What was this? It scared me a little bit that I could have such a reaction to a man that I had just met.

I followed Whitney through the tables and into the bathroom. She spun around, narrowing her eyes at me. "What are you doing? I said I wanted Lane, and you're throwing goo-goo eyes at him. Don't think I haven't noticed!" She was practically melting me with her glaring eyes.

I just stared at her, confused. "I've been talking to Kent all night. I've never thrown any eyes anywhere." I wasn't even sure what goo-goo eyes looked like. I had never seen Whitney like this before.

She just stood there looking at me. "I think I have a really good shot with Lane. Don't blow this for me."

I couldn't think straight right now. Whitney was coming off as slightly crazy and possessive, something I had never seen before. Lane was acting interested in me, and even while I was headed here, he was touching my hand. What was I supposed to do? I had been friends with Whitney for five years and had only just met Lane. Thinking about it like that, it made the choice clear.

I nodded. "Of course, Whitney. I'm not even interested. Maybe he's the one who wanted to try us both out?" I suggested this as a way out, even though I could feel the burn of the lie on my face.

Whitney stopped touching up her makeup in the mirror at that. "Oh, my gosh. He's just playing me! I can't believe it!" She slammed her lipstick down on the counter. "I'll show him."

My head was reeling from the emotional display I had just seen. *What the hell,* I thought as I turned around slowly to follow her back out. This whole night was turning out to be so exhausting.

I returned to the table and grabbed the shot glass in front of my seat. Then, throwing away all my cares, I downed Kent's as well. I wiped my mouth and noticed everyone staring at me. At this point in the night, I couldn't care less.

My head was buzzing, but I kept on drinking. I didn't bother trying to talk to Kent anymore, and Whitney had gone over the top flirting with Lane. I was trying to figure out how that was "showing him", but my brain was too numb to figure it out.

By the end of the night, I could barely manage to stand, let alone walk straight. I laid my head down on the table, feeling drained.

"Do you guys need a ride back?" I could hear Lane asking Whitney.

"No, thanks, I'll get a taxi. I don't think Abigail could walk the few blocks home tonight. *What* has gotten into her?" Whitney wondered.

I felt a hand on my back and then Lane's voice was in my ear. "Are you going to be okay tonight?"

I could feel myself drifting already, and all I managed was a moan. He sighed and stood up. "The least we can do is help her out to the taxi."

Whitney agreed to that, not really having another choice, and I felt arms around me, lifting me up. We walked outside where the cool air revived me a little bit. My mouth felt dry and my head was spinning when I looked around. We were on the sidewalk in front of The Den. Whitney was trying to flag down a taxi and Kent stood a couple feet away, looking at his phone. Lane had his arm around my waist, holding me up.

"Are you okay?" he asked, looking down at me.

"I'll make it. Probably not for a few days though." I was not looking forward to tomorrow's colossal hangover.

Lane laughed at that. "Yeah, I don't think I've ever seen someone drink quite so much at one time. This was quite a first date."

I scoffed at that. "This was *not* a date. I only just met you. You're crazy." It occurred to me that I should step away from him. He was probably getting all sorts of wrong ideas.

I took a step and wobbled. Why was the ground spinning so much? I could feel the nausea rising, and I covered my mouth with my hand, moaning. I couldn't handle throwing up outside in front of two strangers.

Lane turned me toward him and pushed my head to his shoulders. "Shh, Abby. Close your eyes and take slow, deep breaths. In and out. There you go."

Surprisingly, it worked. The rolling nausea eased back down. "Thank you," I whispered. I heard Whitney's heels clicking toward us and heard her huff.

"If you're quite through, our taxi is here," she said. I could just imagine the look on her face now. She was probably royally pissed at Lane holding me.

He helped me into the back of the cab. "Good night, you two," he said, shutting the door.

The taxi started driving away, and I kept my eyes on Lane until he disappeared. Since we only lived a few blocks away, the ride didn't take long. But it felt like forever when I sensed the hostility coming at me from Whitney.

I was able to make it up the elevator and to our apartment by keeping one hand on the wall. Whitney didn't even wait for me. She just walked ahead, slamming the door shut before I reached it. I groaned. This night did get worse.

I opened the door and stepped in, heading toward the kitchen. I needed water and Tylenol. A lot of water. A ten-gallon bucket of water. What I got instead was Whitney waiting for me.

She was leaning against the counter, her arms folded across her chest. "So…not interested in him, huh?"

I shook my head. I was too tired for this. "Don't be like this, Whitney."

"Like what?" She feigned innocence. "You're supposed to be my best friend, but I turn around for two seconds and you're all over my guy!"

I felt a flash of anger. "Your guy? You *just* met him hours ago! What, are you two *together* now?" I went to the pantry and got a couple bottles of water, then to the cabinet above the refrigerator for the Tylenol. Turning to Whitney, I sighed. "Look, this is stupid. We shouldn't be fighting about someone we've only just met. Please, let's just forget about all this. You can have him if you really want him that badly. Let's just not fight anymore."

Whitney sniffed and looked away. "Yeah, well, I don't want a guy that throws himself at any girl he sees, anyway."

I stiffened up, slightly offended that I was just lumped into the category of *any girl*. Taking a deep breath, I blew it out slowly through my nose, calming down. I just wanted to be over this. Plus, I wasn't sure how I would feel if she couldn't accept Lane's interest in me. "Okay. I'm exhausted, so I'm going to bed. Good night." I went to my room, getting my pajamas on before taking some Tylenol and guzzling a bottle of water. Then, I flopped onto the bed, waiting for sleep.

My dream was very strange. It seemed to be quick flashes of things. Cars racing down roads, people walking by me like I didn't even exist. Lane was even there. He stood in front of me, brushing my hair away from my face. "I've never met anyone like you. You interest me." His words echoed our earlier conversation. Then he morphed into my mother. She was leaning over me, as if I were lying down. "I love you, sweetie. Wake up. Please, wake up." Those words echoed in my head. *Wake up. Wake up.*

I woke up, gasping. I was clammy with sweat and my heart was racing. *What in the hell?* I thought to myself. That dream was extremely bizarre. It felt like there was some sort of warning in it. Rubbing my eyes, I sat up. The light was streaming in brightly.

I looked at the clock, my jaw dropping. It was one in the afternoon. How did I sleep so late?

I got up and dressed, ready for some coffee. I hadn't planned on doing much today, even if I hadn't slept half of it away. I turned on the coffee maker and took the creamer out of the refrigerator. After making a cup, I sat on the couch and called my mom. Seeing her in my dream made me realize we hadn't spoken in a while. In fact, I couldn't remember the last time we talked. I frowned at that, listening to the ringing. But it went to her voicemail.

"Well, that blows," I muttered as I put the phone down and drank my coffee.

I finally got up. I needed to straighten up my room. I grabbed my skirt off the floor, getting my keys out of the front pocket. I heard a crinkling noise in the other pocket and found a folded-up paper there. I was sure it wasn't mine. I opened it and saw it was a note.

Abby,

If you ever need someone to talk to.
I'm here.

Lane

His phone number was written at the bottom. I didn't even know what to think. Why would he write this? When did he even put it in my pocket?

Did he feel me up when he put the note there? My cheeks started burning at the thought. This guy just thought highly of himself, didn't he? "I'll show him," I said. But for some reason, instead of throwing the note in the trash, I found myself shoving it in the bottom of my purse.

I spent the rest of the weekend being lazy. Normally, I tried to stay productive, but after my crazy Friday night, I was just over it. Whitney was still acting miffed at me, even though she said she was fine. I was looking forward to getting back to work on Monday.

On Sunday, I got out the manuscript that I had brought home with me on Friday. Frustratingly enough, I couldn't find the focus I needed to read it and mark it up. Eventually, I just put it back.

I ended up going to bed early just to get the day over with. I pulled the covers up to my chin, rolling to my side to get comfortable. All I could think was that I didn't want to have any more weird dreams. But since last night had been okay, I just chalked it up to an alcohol-induced dream.

I sighed and stretched out. *What is going on?* I thought. But deep down, I knew. Lane had gotten into my head. I had ignored it for two days, but it was hard to keep doing that. So, in the safety of my room, I closed my eyes and let Lane into my thoughts.

I recalled the way he looked at me after he saved me from the car, asking if they could join us. His smile at me and how he looked at me when we were waiting at the bar. He had woken something in me that I hadn't realized was even there. I was twenty-five years old and I had dated before, but nobody had ever made me feel this way. I never knew before what I was missing. And we hadn't even been on a date! It was an impromptu joining, only because the careless driver of the car had brought us together. We hardly even talked that night. I wished I could share this with Whitney but given what had happened Friday night with her reaction to Lane's interest in me, I knew it wasn't a good idea.

I closed my eyes and didn't open them again until Monday morning. I woke up to my alarm, bright and early. I got dressed in a knee-length black skirt and tucked in a pearly white satin shirt. I slipped on some black heels and looked at myself in the mirror.

"Yes," I said softly. "Power outfit to power through Monday." I glanced at my face. "Okay, after I do something with my face and hair." I finished my makeup, trying to keep it light. After pulling my hair up into a ponytail, I packed up my briefcase and left the apartment to get my car.

I arrived at work and got to my desk. Sitting down, I straightened up a few picture frames and unloaded the manuscript from my briefcase.

"Coffee next," I sighed to myself. I turned my computer on and then headed to the break room. Another editor, Julie, was already there.

"Hey, Abigail!" she exclaimed. Julie was always very enthusiastic, even this early in the morning. "How was your weekend? Anything exciting happen?"

I sighed and poured coffee into my cup, sweetening it up with sugar and creamer. "Oh, it wasn't too bad, Julie. Whitney and I went out on Friday night and met a couple guys." I saw her eyes brighten at that and quickly tried to head her off. "But they definitely weren't keepers."

Julie deflated, seeming upset that she couldn't gab about guys with me. But, honestly, she just tried too hard. She was in her late forties, had been divorced for four months, and was now acting like she was in her twenties again, needing to gossip about everything. Men were her favorite topic right now. I had a feeling her biological clock was ticking to find a new husband.

"Anyways," I went on, "I just spent the rest of the weekend at home, not doing anything. How about you?" I took a sip of coffee, knowing Julie would jump at the chance to talk about herself.

"Well, I went on a date with a guy named Brian. He was very handsome. We went to dinner and I'm not sure where I went wrong, but he took me home after and didn't even kiss me good night!"

I took another sip of coffee, taking in Julie's sad expression. As much as she got on my nerves, I couldn't help but feel sorry for her now. I laid a hand on her shoulder. "Hey, it's okay, Julie. Maybe he's just not a kiss on the first date kind of guy."

She looked reassured at that and perked up. "Yeah, maybe you're right! I'm going to go see if he texted me!" She hurried off.

I rolled my eyes. "Wow. Someone please shoot me if I turn into that," I pleaded to the universe. I finished my coffee and washed the cup out, setting it on the dish rack to dry.

Walking back to the office area, I said hello to a few co-workers as I passed by them. Then, I was at my desk. *Time to get my head in the game*, I thought. I pulled my manuscript in front of me and started to read. I made notes in a notebook, marking pages and places.

When I looked up, I saw it was time for my lunch break. "Finally!" I stretched out my back, feeling it pop in a few places.

I headed toward the break room with my lunch bag. Julie was there along with a handful of others. Sitting down, I took out my lunch and started eating. I only had thirty minutes, so I tried to make the most of it. Everyone else in here was older than me, so I didn't have a lot in common with them. I had been lucky to get hired on here right after college. It had been a coveted position and I was told there were a lot of applicants.

I listened to the small talk but didn't participate much. My thoughts stupidly kept drifting back to Lane. *There's nothing to even think of! You met him once, he flirted with you. And there's no chance of seeing him again!* I scrunched up my trash angrily.

I stood up to go back to my desk. I slowed down and then stopped when I reached it. Nothing seemed out of place, but at the same time, something seemed messed up. Like it was moved and then put back, but not exactly as it was before. *Weird*, I thought, because I had no idea what the problem was. *I just need a nap. Or maybe caffeine. Surely one of those will work.*

I got back up to get a Diet Coke from the vending machine. I took it back to my desk. "Okay," I said to myself. "Time to get some real work done."

Opening the manuscript to my last spot, I started to read and take notes again. I had gotten halfway through the chapter when I turned the page and saw something that made my blood run cold. I read it once, then twice. Looking up, I glanced at everyone in the office to see if this was a joke. Nobody was paying any attention to me though. They were all just doing their own work.

What the hell is this? I thought. Because this was most certainly not part of the historical fiction story I was reading. But it was in there, right between two other paragraphs, like it belonged there.

I ran my fingers over the words, trying to make sense of it all. I had to read them again.

If you're reading this, you've been in a coma for almost five years now. We're trying a new technique. We don't know where this message will end up in your dream, but we hope we're getting through. Please wake up! We miss you.

Chapter Two

This was insane. This wasn't possible. I couldn't figure out how to react to what I had just read. This was like something out of a sci-fi movie. It just didn't make sense.

I sat back in my chair, trying to wrap my brain around it. Maybe it was a mistake? Could the author have actually typed this into his book? I shook my head. No, that didn't make sense either; the book was set in the 1700's. But I had to find out.

I stood up, separating the page from the rest of the stack. I started toward my manager's office but hesitated before I could knock. *I can't just give the page away*, I thought. This was too weird to just pass on and forget about it.

I turned and went to the copy machine. Sliding the page in, I pressed the copy button and waited while a new paper slid out of the back. I folded it up small and slipped it into my skirt pocket.

Now I'm ready. I made my way back to my manager's office and knocked on the door.

"Come in," I heard her say.

I opened the door and saw Lauren Cross sitting behind her desk, engaged with her computer screen, typing fast on her keyboard.

"What's up?" she asked, without looking away from her screen.

I hesitated again, feeling foolish. "Well, um, I was going through my manuscript and saw something really strange."

Now Lauren did look at me. "Strange how?"

I held out the page toward her. "Here. It's a few lines down."

Lauren took the page and started reading. As she read, her mouth turned into a frown. She got to the bottom and flipped the page over, as if she expected to read more. Turning it back, she skimmed it again before looking at me.

"I'm not sure what part you're talking about, Abigail." Lauren held the page out. "Point it out to me."

I swallowed. I leaned over to her, showing her where the bizarre paragraph was.

Lauren looked down at the page and then back at me. "Abigail, that's just the story. It flows with the rest of it and there's nothing out of place about it."

I stared at her, confused. *Can she not see it?* I wondered to myself. I took the paper, looked it over. The note seemed to jump off the page at me. *I'm going crazy. No other explanation.*

"You know what, you're right. I must have read it wrong." I stood up, trying to retreat gracefully.

Lauren narrowed her eyes at me. "Is everything okay, Abigail?" she inquired.

No, it's not. "Yes, it's okay. Just been a long day, and I didn't sleep well last night," I lied to her.

I exited the office, making my way back to my desk. I considered asking others if they saw what I did, but I didn't want to risk them not seeing it, and then the office would be gossiping about me.

Instead, I would take my copy home and ask Whitney. Maybe she would have an idea. I put the original back in its spot. I looked at my watch, amazed at how my day had turned upside down so fast.

I made it through the rest of the day knowing I couldn't pay the attention I needed to at the story I was reading, thanks to that strange note. I would probably have to do this same section again tomorrow.

Five o'clock finally came, and I heaved a sigh of relief. I raced home, bursting to be able to talk to Whitney about my strange day.

I opened the front door. "Whitney?" I called out. She was usually home before I was. "You here?"

Making my way to the living room, I saw Whitney on the couch, watching television.

"Hey, did you hear me calling you?"

"Yup," was all Whitney said as she changed channels. She didn't even look up at me.

I couldn't believe this. How long was this grudge going to last?

I sat down in the recliner beside the couch, looking at Whitney as she studiously ignored me. *Well A for effort, I guess*, I thought.

"Look, I need your help with something." I pulled out the copy I had hidden in my pocket. I felt like it had been burning a hole there all day. "It's hard to explain. Just read this and see if anything weird jumps out at you." I held out the page.

Whitney looked at me skeptically, but took it. She took about five seconds to scan it and handed it back, barely glancing at me. "Nope, I don't see anything."

I stared at her in amazement. I couldn't believe how she was acting toward me. Still!

"Are you kidding me, Whitney? How are you going to sit there and treat me like this? I needed your help, I feel like I'm going through a crisis, and you're *still* pissed because some guy you *barely* met and know might *actually* like me better than you?" I threw up my hands in frustration and stood up. "Well, screw you, Whitney. I'm glad to know some stranger is more important than your best friend."

Whitney's mouth was gaping open. I'm sure I surprised her; I had never acted like this before. I was the quiet friend who never acted out. Whitney was the loud one who was never scared to voice her opinion.

But today my world had turned upside down and I needed help. I didn't have time for someone who was angry and jealous. I had to solve this problem.

I stormed off to my room, slamming the door. It felt good to physically let off some anger. I flopped onto my bed, lying on my stomach.

Pulling out the page, I examined the message again. *A coma for five years? There's no way this is possible.* I had no explanation for why nobody else could see the note, though. Of course, I had only showed two people. And I couldn't be sure one of them had even read it. I rolled my eyes.

A few minutes later there was a knock on my door. Whitney popped her head in, looking contrite. "Can I come in?"

I sighed and sat up. "Yeah, sure."

Whitney came in and sat on my desk chair, twiddling her fingers. *She must be nervous*, I thought.

She combed her hair back behind her ears and cleared her throat. "I thought about what you said," she started, her eyes darting around. "It's not fair to treat you this way over some guy I don't even know." She finally looked me in the eyes. "You were right. I was jealous." She gave me a small smile. "I guess since I wanted him, I just assumed he would want me too. It never occurred to me that he might be interested in you instead."

I let out a huff, annoyed. "Just because you don't get what you want, you can't take it out on me."

Whitney nodded. "I know. I'm really sorry."

There was the apology I was looking for. "Apology accepted." I felt a little better now.

"Maybe I could take another look at your paper? I promise to really read it this time." Whitney looked at me hopefully.

I handed it to her and watched as she read it. I could feel my hope deflating as I saw her pass the spot I knew the message to be at.

Whitney shook her head. "I don't see anything. What is it that's scaring you?"

I took the page back. Where did I even begin? I recounted my story of what had happened, what the note said, and how Whitney was now the second person who didn't even see it at all.

Whitney's mouth was wide open by the end of my story. I couldn't tell if she believed me or not.

"Um, what? How is this even possible? I mean, surely it's someone's idea of a joke!" she said, incredulous.

"Yeah, but how am I going to get anyone to believe me if nobody else can see what I see? A coma? No way! Right? I mean, I remember my whole life!" By this time, I was up, pacing around my room.

Whitney quietly said, "I believe you."

That stopped me in my tracks. "Really? You do?" Hope surged through me.

"Of course, I do. You're my best friend. I'm always here for you." She held out her hand to me and I took it.

"Thank you," I whispered. It felt good to have my friend back.

Whitney inhaled, fanning her eyes. "Okay! Now let's figure this out, so I won't start crying." She let out a laugh.

I laughed too, since I had wanted to cry myself. "I don't even know where to start," I admitted.

Whitney thought for a minute. "Well, the note says five years, right? Where were you five years ago?"

Five years? "I was still in college." I thought back to that time in my life. "The only thing I can think of is that's when my migraines started."

Whitney frowned. "Really? No idea of the cause?"

I shook my head. "No. They just started one day. Medicine doesn't really help. And it's always on one side of my head." I pointed to the middle of the left side of my head.

"Hmmm. Interesting, but a lot of people get migraines," Whitney pointed out. "I'm not sure if that's important or not."

"I'm not sure either." I really had no idea what could help me.

Whitney got up. "It's getting late. I'm going to order pizza for dinner. Sound good?"

I nodded absentmindedly. I needed some time to process all of this.

By the time the pizza arrived, I was having zero luck. No new ideas had come to me. I joined Whitney in the kitchen, eating some pizza and drinking a few beers. Whitney was drinking wine.

"What if this is some big joke your boss is playing on you?" Whitney asked while chewing on a bite.

"No, that doesn't make sense." I shook my head. "You can't see the note either. I have a feeling nobody but me *can* see it."

I was starting to feel despair. What was I supposed to do now? Suddenly, my appetite was completely gone. I felt like I was going to choke if I tried to eat anymore. Nobody could help me. I was on my own.

I stood up from the table, too anxious to sit still anymore. "I need to get some air." I was starting to feel frantic. The air itself was smothering me.

Heading to my room, I quickly changed out of my work clothes and put on jeans, a t-shirt, and sneakers. I grabbed my purse and left the room.

Whitney was standing in the hallway, a concerned look on her face. "What's going on, Abigail? Do you want me to come with you?"

"No, stay here. I need fresh air and to walk around and think." I couldn't stay here in this place right now. I felt like I could barely breathe.

I practically raced out and headed toward the elevator. Realizing it would be too slow for my needs, I turned instead for the stairs. By this time, I was trying to suck in air, imagining that there was no oxygen left for me.

And why not? I thought, making my way outside. *Apparently, this isn't real.* I'm *not real. Why should I need to breathe then?*

In the back of my head, where rationality ruled, I knew I could breathe fine. I could feel my chest rising and falling, my heart beating fast. Somehow, I kept putting one foot in front of the other, not paying attention to where I was going, just knowing that I had to *go go go*.

A squeal of tires and a car horn blaring brought me back to reality. I had stepped into the street and now a car was swerving to avoid me, the horn warning me of danger. I could see the driver inside, anger and panic on his face, his arm waving around while he yelled at me, presumably.

I gasped and jumped back to the corner to safety. What was I doing? *What is wrong with me?* I wondered. *Nothing has changed. You're still you. Abigail Hendricks. Twenty-five years old. Editor. College graduate. Daughter of Ed and Sherry Hendricks.*

I backed up to the store that was on the corner and slid down the wall. I hadn't realized I was crying until I tried to take my phone out of my purse and could barely see. My hands were shaking as I tried to dial my mom's number.

Pick up, I pleaded silently. *Please, pick up, please.* But the ringing never stopped. I never heard my mom's voice telling me hello until the voicemail picked up.

"Mommy? Please call me." I was bawling into the phone now, and my nose was running. "I really need to talk to you. Please." I hung up, unsure of what else I could do.

I hung my head in my hands, trying to calm myself down. I couldn't do anything if I couldn't get control of myself.

"Miss, are you okay?" I heard a man asking.

"I'm fine, thanks," I said loudly, not bothering to lift my head.

I thought I could hear a woman pleading with him, and then I saw a hand putting a few dollar bills by my feet. I snorted. *I guess they think I'm homeless.* I felt wrung out and ready to go home.

"Abby?"

I froze, still looking down. This was *not* happening. Of all the people to see me like this!

I looked up and saw Lane standing over me. *My night got worse*, I thought sarcastically.

As soon as I looked up, I saw his expression change from curiosity to concern. He took in my red and blotchy face, which I could feel was slightly swollen. His eyes raked over my appearance and breathlessness.

He slowly knelt in front of me. "Abby?" he repeated. "What happened? Are you okay?" He took one of my hands in his. It felt a lot better than I thought it should have.

"I'm okay," I whispered. "I just had a really rough night and I needed to get out."

Lane rubbed his thumb against my hand. "Must have been some night to have you out here like this. Want to talk about it?"

I shook my head. I couldn't talk about what I had seen with anyone else. People who saw what nobody else could see got sent straight to the looney bin. Plus, I didn't want to scare Lane off. A small thrill had run through me at seeing him again.

"Can I walk you home then? That is, if you were wanting to go there," Lane offered.

I nodded. "Yes, please, that would be great."

He tightened his grip on my hand and stood up, helping to pull me up after him. He put his other hand on my arm, steadying me. He peered into my eyes, and the concern I saw there made them well again.

Lane scrunched his eyebrows together and pulled me in, holding me tightly. "Hey, it'll be okay. Whatever's going on, I can help you."

I leaned into him, resting my head on his shoulder, feeling his hand rub my back soothingly. This felt nice. I didn't want to move. In fact, I didn't think I could move. My head was starting to get dizzy and a familiar throbbing had begun in the left side of my head, shimmering spots flaring in my vision.

"Oh, no," I said, stepping back from Lane. "Please hurry and help me home."

Noticing the change in my tone of voice, Lane searched my face, but didn't say anything. He grabbed my purse from me, put his right arm around my waist and with the other, held onto my left arm to support me.

We had only gone half a block when the pain burst through my head, causing me to gasp and stumble.

"Ahhh!" I cried out and held out a hand to break my fall.

But I didn't fall. Lane was holding me close, supporting me. He moved me to the side of the building and lifted my face to his. Even that tiny bit of movement made fire flash through the left side of my head repeatedly.

"Stop, stop, stop," I begged, squeezing my eyes shut. "It's just a migraine. I need to get home. Oh, God, please get me home."

Lane was sounding extremely worried when he answered. "Okay, Abby. Here, just slide down so you can sit and I'll call a cab so you don't have to walk. Can you do that?"

I couldn't even nod a yes to him. I was frozen in the grip of my migraine, and all I could do was let it run its course. I felt Lane helping me back down to the ground, where I slumped over, my cheek pressed to the cool concrete.

When I opened my eyes, I was alone. And it was daylight. I sat up. *That jerk just left me here?* I thought furiously. *Okay,* not *calling him, ever! I am throwing away his note when I get home!*

I stood up, realizing I didn't know where I was. Panicking, I looked around, turning in place. I saw no cars, no people. Just streets, buildings, and a payphone across the street.

Where am I? I wondered.

"Hello?" I called out. "Hello! Anybody here?" I was going to throttle Lane for dumping me here if I ever saw him again. Which I wouldn't. Because I was never going to call him.

Speaking of calls. "I may as well call Whitney to come get me," I grumbled, as I walked to the corner to cross it. Then we could get drunk and complain about Lane together.

I neared the payphone and stopped before I entered. I didn't have my purse. Which probably didn't mean anything as I never carried cash on me, anyway.

"Shit," I said, kicking the booth that the phone was in. I turned around and yelled as loudly as I could, "Hello! Where is everybody?"

The phone rang, causing me to scream and jump around. I just stared at it, unsure of what to do. Slowly, I made my way to the door and looked at it. A minute passed by, and still it rang.

This wasn't normal. I turned in a circle again, wondering where I was.

And still, the phone rang.

I sighed and went inside of the booth. I had to summon the courage to lift the receiver to my ear.

"Hello?" I said quietly.

If I was expecting to hear Lane or Whitney, then I was way off. All I heard was beeping.

"If this is someone's idea of a joke, then you lose! Ha, ha! This isn't funny!" I shouted into the phone.

I heard the beeping go faster. What was this, a countdown to something? I was no fool, I had seen movies. I searched the inside of the phone booth but saw nothing that looked like a bomb.

I let out the breath I was holding and heard the beeping speed up as I inhaled again. *What?* I was so confused. I held my breath and the beeping slowed down. I started to feel my heartbeat in my chest. *Ba-bump. Ba-bump. Ba-bump.*

Why was the beeping on the phone matching my heartbeat? This was getting too weird. I hung up the phone and exited the booth. Looking around, I still had no idea where I was. I might as well pick a direction and stick with it and hope that I found someone for help.

The sun was ahead of me, seeming to be on the way to setting. *Why couldn't I have been stranded with sunglasses?* I thought, shielding my eyes against the glare.

The light was so dazzling that it seemed to be draining the color out of everything else. Wait. The color *was* leaving everything. I was being left in a world that was shades of white and gray, with the sun blinding me. All I could do was cover my eyes and try to move forward.

Soon enough, that proved to be too much to do. The sun seemed to have grown. It covered the sky in front of me, blinding me. I tried to find shade in a doorway and sat down, covering my face with my hands.

"Abigail? Can you hear me?"

I tried to look beyond my hands, but the light was too bright. I groaned loudly at the piercing pain in my head that it was causing.

I heard someone in front of me. "Turn that light over there off. I bet it's hurting her head."

Somehow the sun got darker. I peered between my fingers and saw part of Whitney's face. I felt like crying. She found me!

"Whitney!" My voice sounded garbled, like I hadn't used it in months. "You found me!" I closed my eyes again, relieved.

"What is she talking about?" I heard Whitney ask.

"I have no idea."

Wait, was that Lane? The jerk who abandoned me?

"Go away, Lane! You left me in nowhere and I had to answer the phone and find my own way back." I wasn't even sure what I was saying. I just knew I had to tell Lane off and put him in his place.

"What?" asked Whitney.

"I have no idea what she's talking about," said Lane. "I helped her to sit down and she passed out. We took a cab here and you know the rest."

I waved my hand in his direction. "Liar," I slurred. "You left me. I was alone. There was nobody else but me. Why did you leave me, Lane?" I felt a few tears squeeze out, which I tried to stop.

"Oh, Abby." I felt Lane take my hand. "I would never leave you if you needed me."

"Good," I whispered, too tired to try to talk normally. "I was really sad when I thought you left me."

I tried opening my eyes again and saw Lane in front of me. His brown eyes were staring into mine. His hand was holding onto mine and the other was brushing my hair back. I leaned into the hand on my face and sighed.

"Thank you," I whispered. "How out of it was I?"

Lane cracked a smile at me, making my heart stutter. "Well, you scared me a little. You passed out on the street and didn't come around until just now. You were saying some pretty weird things." His hand brushed my cheek again.

I turned my head to find Whitney and felt nausea rising up my throat. I groaned, "I need Whitney. A girl. Not you. Go away."

Lane laughed and moved away, Whitney taking his place beside me. She wiped my face off with a damp washcloth. That made me feel better.

I looked at her again. "You have no idea how happy I am to see you."

"I'm not leaving you, Abigail," she promised. "I'm right here, not going anywhere."

"Okay, good. Because I think I am about to throw up." My stomach was not obeying my commands to settle down. I leaned forward, my stomach starting to heave on its own.

Fortunately, Whitney was prepared with a trash can for me. I leaned into it, emptying my stomach's contents. My stomach convulsed until there was nothing left for it to bring up. I was left hanging over the trash can, spitting out the saliva that kept gathering in my mouth.

"Whitney?" I whispered, still leaning forward.

"Yeah? What do you need?" Whitney replied.

"Is Lane still here? Did he see me vomit?"

Silence. I felt Whitney shifting on the seat beside me. "Yeah, Abigail, he's still here."

Kill me. I couldn't believe he just saw me like that. *Great.* At least my head wasn't pounding anymore.

I could sit up on my own now. We were in our living room. I was sitting on the couch. Whitney sat next to me and Lane was in the recliner to our left. The trash can was in front of me. I put the lid on it before its contents could offend anybody's nose.

Whitney stood up, wiping her hands on her pants. "I'm going to take the trash out and get you some water, Abigail. I'll be right back." She patted me on the shoulder and grabbed the trash can before heading back into the kitchen.

I was feeling so self-conscious that I could barely look at Lane. Luckily for me, he was the one to make a move. He stood up and took Whitney's spot beside me on the couch.

"How are you?" he asked.

I exhaled loudly, leaning on my side to be able to look at him. "I'm feeling like I went through the ringer." I didn't even want to think about what made me run out tonight, let alone the crazy vision I had while I was apparently passed out.

Lane picked up one of my hands in-between both of his. "Whatever happened, I'm here."

I just looked at him, perplexed. "Why?"

Lane got a surprised look on his face. "What do you mean, why?"

"Like, why? Why do you care, why do you want to help, why do you want to be here?" It was so exhausting trying to keep up with Lane's motives.

"Oh, Abby," Lane said, scooting closer to me. "Don't you remember me telling you? You interest me." He laid a hand on my cheek, which I couldn't help but lean into. "I've never met anyone like you. I want to know you better. To make you feel safer than you have been feeling. Ever since we met the other night, you've been on my mind."

My breath hitched. I've never had someone declare any sort of feelings for me before. Certainly not such strong feelings. It was a novelty for me.

"I can't stop thinking about you, either," I whispered. The expression lighting up Lane's face was enough to satisfy me. I now knew for sure that Lane was interested in me. I couldn't help but wonder if it was petty of me to secretly gloat that I was right, and Lane liked me rather than Whitney.

I leaned my head back on the couch. "I think I just need to sleep now." Everything seemed to be crashing down on me at once, and I couldn't deal with it where I was right now. Definitely not with someone who didn't know my secret.

That was another thing. Did I explain everything that had happened to me to Lane? Except, I couldn't. I could only imagine what he would think after I told him everything that had occurred. I didn't want to scare him away.

I stood up and swayed, and Lane was immediately there, helping me to stay upright.

I pushed his hands away. "I'm fine, I can do this," I insisted.

Lane looked like he was about to protest, but Whitney chose then to walk back into the living room to join us.

She looked back and forth between us before taking control. "Okay, Lane, you go. Abigail, I'm going to get you to bed."

Lane stepped toward me. "Let me just say good night, please."

I nodded at Whitney, who headed toward our two bedrooms, down the hallway.

Lane kept his distance until Whitney disappeared, and then he stepped closer to me, leaving no space between us.

"Please, let me help you," Lane pleaded.

"Do you even know what you're wanting to do? I know you say you want to know me, make me feel safe, and that I interest you. But you don't really know me. Not really." I shook my head. "We met days ago, and we didn't even talk then. You were too busy with Whitney. And I was talking to your brother, you know, Kent?"

Lane narrowed his eyes at me and smirked. My breath caught, I hadn't seen this before. *Did he have to be so damn good looking?* I asked myself.

"You won't scare me off," Lane remarked.

I took a shaky breath. "Okay." That's really all I could say. I didn't want to argue with him anymore. This day had taken all the energy out of me.

Lane smiled at me. "Well, okay then." He took my hand, bent down, and kissed it.

I was not expecting that at all. And yet, it seemed totally appropriate.

Whitney conveniently came into the room and broke up whatever kind of moment we had been having.

Lane nodded at me, waved at Whitney, and left our apartment.

I looked at Whitney. "Let's talk about this weirdness tomorrow. This night has been too much for me."

She nodded and put an arm around my shoulders, steering me to my room. "I've laid out your pajamas, and your sheets are pulled back. I will turn off your light for you when you're ready."

My eyes teared again as I hugged her quickly. "Thank you," I said. "I couldn't be here without you."

Whitney was quick to push her emotions down, but not before I saw her swipe a tear off her cheek. "Just get in bed, so I can go lie down, too."

I changed out of my clothes and into the pajamas Whitney had laid out for me. I had barely touched my head to the pillow before she had turned off the lights and I was drifting off to sleep.

Chapter Three

I rolled over and groaned. The light was painfully bright against my closed eyes. I opened them a sliver and immediately scrunched them closed again.

My head was throbbing, reminding me of the slightly insane events that had taken place last night.

I groaned again. "Please let me have dreamed all that," I pleaded. Had I really hallucinated an entire dream world whose only inhabitant was me? Obviously, I had just succumbed to the pain that the migraine had given me, and I was also feeling overwhelmed about the note.

I slowly sat up, wincing at my sore muscles. I stayed like that for a minute, willing myself the energy to get all the way out of bed. Finally, I made it up and stretched, working out all the kinks in my back and neck.

I put on my slippers and headed toward the kitchen. There were already heavenly smells coming from there, drawing me closer.

Whitney was at the stove, flipping bacon over to its other side. There was a jug of orange juice on the counter plus a pot of coffee heating up.

She looked up and saw me. She motioned to the orange juice with her spatula. "Have something to drink. I bet you need it."

I poured a cup of coffee and added sugar and creamer to it. Taking a deep sniff, I closed my eyes and sighed, "Just what I needed." I lifted the cup to my lips, but before I could take a drink, I saw the time on the microwave and let out a small shriek.

"Oh my God, Whitney, why didn't you wake me up? I was supposed to be at work an hour ago!" I was about to launch out of my chair before I saw Whitney smile.

"It's okay! I texted your boss on your phone last night and told her you were taking a couple of sick days for your migraine."

I relaxed back into my seat, wishing for my thudding heart to relax too. "Thanks a lot, Whitney. You're a lifesaver."

She flipped the bacon onto a plate and then added eggs in the pan, scrambling them. "No problem. I figured after yesterday you needed some time off."

I nodded and took a drink of my coffee, savoring the rich taste. I could use some time off work. That's what caused so much of my trouble in the first place. I had so much to think about that I probably wouldn't be able to get any work done at all.

Whitney served the bacon and eggs, along with biscuits that had been in the oven. I looked it over appreciatively, knowing this was Whitney's way of mothering me. I ate too much of everything, but I felt no guilt. I was sure I would stress it all out later.

I helped Whitney clear the dishes and then we took our coffees to the living room. Sitting on opposite ends of the couch, I felt like I could finally talk about the events of last night.

I launched into an explanation of what had prompted me to run out in the first place. The helplessness and aloneness I felt, because I couldn't truly turn to anyone for help. How I felt half-crazy just thinking about it.

Whitney stayed quiet and watched me while I talked, drinking her coffee and nodding occasionally. It felt good to unburden myself to her.

Whitney furrowed her eyebrows, thinking. "How did Lane find you though?"

"I'm honestly not sure. I think it was a coincidence. I was sitting at a corner and he came up to me."

"Pretty major coincidence," Whitney said, raising her eyebrows in speculation. "He just happened to be there?"

I shrugged. "I totally agree. But all in all, I'm happy he was there to help. I'm not sure I would've made it home otherwise."

Whitney smirked at me. "Oh, yeah? Were you gonna go all damsel-in-distress on him? Gonna have those big, strong arms carry you home?"

I rolled my eyes and laughed. "Wow, Whitney. No, that was definitely not the plan!"

Whitney shifted on the couch, getting into a more comfortable position. "Seriously, though. He does seem very into you. How do you feel about that?"

I looked at her closely to make sure there weren't any hard feelings left about Lane. But she seemed genuinely interested.

Taking a deep breath, I said, "It scares me, to be honest. The guys I've dated in the past were never serious. And then here comes this guy who I met days ago and he's already more serious about a relationship than any of those other guys ever were." I rubbed my hands on my face, trying to think. "Is that insane? Does that make him sweet or creepy?"

Whitney smiled at me. "Girl, just go with it. It's easy enough to get rid of him if you want to. I say ride it out until you're done with it."

"That's true. And I'll tell him you wanted to do a double date with his brother."

Whitney threw a pillow at me. "Oh, very funny! I'll pass on that, thanks."

I laughed, throwing the pillow back. It felt so good to sit here and joke around with Whitney. But I couldn't entirely forget about my situation.

I sobered up quickly, my smile dropping.

Whitney noticed the change in my demeanor and asked, "What's wrong? Something else happen? A new note?"

I shook my head. "No. But I didn't tell you everything that happened last night."

I told Whitney about my dream while I was unconscious. "I was alone, nobody was there. It was so unnerving. I tried to call you, but all I heard on the other end was beeping."

Whitney tilted her head, confused. "Beeping? What kind of beeping?"

I shrugged. "I have no idea. But the weird thing was that it seemed connected to my heartbeat. It sped up, the beeping sped up. Held my breath and it slowed down."

Whitney sat back. "Like…a heart-rate monitor?"

I looked at her, frozen. "No way. Besides, it was just a dream. My brain was making up crazy things."

"You're probably right," Whitney nodded. "I'm sure it was just a crazy migraine dream."

"Yeah," I said slowly. "I was thinking about that stupid note all night. That must be the reason."

So why did that thought make me so uneasy? Surely that's all there was to it?

I shook my head, trying to clear my thoughts. "Okay, we need a new topic. This is starting to depress me."

I got up and went to my purse, grabbing Lane's note from it. Plopping back down on the couch, I handed it to Whitney. "Tell me what you think about that."

Whitney took the note and read it. "Wow. He gave you his number?"

"Yeah. I haven't called him though."

"Why not? You totally should."

"Well, I'm not supposed to make the first move, am I?" I sighed. "I'm hopeless at these things."

Whitney handed back the note. "My opinion? He made a huge move last night. He stayed with you and brought you home. If that's not a first move, I don't know what is."

I considered that. "Okay," I said slowly, "but what do I say?"

"Just ask him out. To dinner. Or coffee. That's a pretty neutral place."

I picked up my phone. "Okay. I can do this." I started to dial. Three numbers in and my fingers were trembling. I slammed the phone down on the coffee table.

"Okay, no. This is a bad idea."

"Oh, no you don't." Whitney grabbed my phone and dialed Lane's number.

"What are you doing?" I was panicking now, trying to grab back my phone. "Stop doing that!"

Whitney grinned, dancing out of my grasp. "This is happening! Don't fight it!" She pushed the phone at me. "It's ringing!"

"What! I can't believe you! That was completely—"

"Hello?"

I froze. Lane had answered.

"What do I say?" I hissed at Whitney.

"Hello?"

Whitney was gesturing at me to say something.

"Hi, Lane? It's Abigail."

"Abby?" Lane's voice warmed up. "How are you?"

"Um, I'm better. I was just calling to say thank you for last night."

"Of course. I'm glad I was around to help you."

Whitney was waving her hands at me again. "Coffee!" she whisper-shouted at me.

"Yeah, so I was wondering if you wanted to meet up for coffee sometime. Maybe later this week?"

"How about today? I'm free."

I looked at Whitney for help. "Today?"

Whitney emphatically nodded her head yes.

"Yes, that's fine."

"Great. I'll come pick you up around eleven."

"Okay. Eleven is fine."

"Sounds good. And Abby? I'm really glad you called. Bye." Lane hung up.

I stared at my phone and then at Whitney. "We have a date today."

Whitney shrieked and clapped her hands. "Yay!"

"I can't believe you made me do that! It was horrifying!"

Whitney laughed. "Hey, it worked. You're seeing him again!"

I felt the panic set in again. "Oh, God, I am." I sank down onto the couch. "What do I do now?"

"Well, first, take a deep breath and calm down. Then, go shower and get ready!"

"Okay. I can do that."

After showering and doing my hair, I went to my closet and stared at my clothes. *Nothing to wear.* I finally chose a pair of jeans, a black shirt, and black flats.

Whitney popped her head in the door. "Oh, cute! That's perfect!"

I let out a relieved breath. At least I had one thing going for me. I went to the living room and started pacing. I don't remember ever being this nervous for a date before. I also don't remember liking a guy this much before, either.

Whitney came in and forced me to sit down. "Breathe, Abigail. It's *just* coffee. You'll be fine."

"You're right. I don't know why I'm so jumpy."

The doorbell rang. I jumped up, my heart pounding. Whitney made a stealthy exit down the hall to her room.

I opened the door and saw Lane standing there. My breath caught in my throat at seeing him. He was wearing jeans, boots, and a green button-up shirt. He looked amazing.

"Hi," I said, a little breathless.

"Hi," he smiled. "You ready?"

I nodded and grabbed my purse. "Ready."

We left down the elevator, not talking. I was feeling pretty awkward about this whole thing. Stepping outside, Lane took my hand in his and directed me toward his car, opening my door for me.

"In you go."

I blushed and sat down. *Breathe, Abigail. It's just a guy, it's just a date. Take it easy.*

Lane got in and we started down the street. "So, you're feeling better? You were pretty out of it."

I nodded. "Yeah. A good night's sleep is all I needed, I guess. Sorry for all the trouble I caused you."

Lane waved his hand at me. "No trouble at all. I'm glad I was there to help."

I was glad he had been there too. Even though it had been extremely embarrassing.

Lane pulled into a trendy little coffee shop and helped me out of the car. Going inside, I noticed they had decorated the place in earth tones and flowers everywhere. There was a counter in front of us that had a display of pastries and muffins that smelled incredible. Tables and couches were spread around the rest of the shop, somehow giving the impression that each place to sit at would give all of the guests their privacy.

We ordered our coffees and some pastries and sat down at a corner table. The shop was about half-full, making me wonder how many of them were skipping out on work like I was.

"So, tell me about yourself. I think I heard you say you're an editor?" Lane asked.

I nodded, picking at my raspberry pastry. "Yes. I work at Voodoo Publishing. I read the manuscripts and I help out with the storylines and check them for all sorts of errors." Errors like life-changing magic notes. My throat felt like it was closing up as I remembered that.

Lane didn't seem to notice my reaction. "Well that seems like a cool job. I used to love reading as a kid, but kind of grew out of it as I got older and discovered other things I could do. Especially after I learned how to drive."

I laughed at that, imagining Lane as a teenager driving around in a truck. I figured he had to be a truck kind of guy. We talked about all sorts of things, and I felt myself relaxing more as time went by. It turned out we had a lot in common, and he had a great sense of humor, making me laugh often.

I was in the middle of a story when I heard my mom say, "I love you, Abigail."

I dropped my cup, spilling coffee everywhere and I jumped out of my seat, scanning the coffee shop for her. *Where was she? I just heard her!*

Lane's voice finally penetrated the fog in my head. "Abigail? Abby? What's going on? Are you all right?"

I turned to him, dazed. He was cleaning up my spill with some napkins and he was looking at me, confused. I felt tears welling up in my eyes, and I attempted to blink them away. *Oh God, I'm going crazy.* I suddenly felt so exhausted. I was tired of hearing and seeing things that only I could hear and see.

"I'm sorry, I can't do this." I bent down to pick up my purse and stood up. "I'll get a taxi back."

I rushed to the door, weaving my way between tables. I could hear Lane calling my name, trying to reach me.

I got outside and practically ran to the street, silently praying for a taxi to come my way. Not seeing any, I started down the sidewalk in the direction we had come from.

A hand grabbed my arm and pulled me around roughly. "What the hell, Abigail?" Lane asked, anger written all over his face.

I took a step back, slightly scared. Shaking my head, I said, "It doesn't matter. I think I'm going mad. You don't need to be around that. Find someone better."

Lane took a step toward me. "But, Abby—"

"I can't. I'm so sorry." I turned around and walked as fast as I could down the street, trying not to draw attention to myself. By now though, I was fully crying, and I could feel my face turning red as I kept wiping at it.

Why was this happening to me? I didn't understand it. I didn't deserve this. And *Lane*, did I really have to freak out in front of him? He probably thought I was crazy now. I would never see him again, not that I could blame him.

It took me over half an hour, but I finally made it back to my apartment. Unlocking the door, I stepped in and saw Whitney in the kitchen, looking uncomfortable. She motioned with her eyes to the living room, as if to tell me to go in there.

I looked in and felt my stomach drop in surprise at seeing Lane in there. He was looking down at his phone, typing something into it.

I heard my text tone go off, loud and clear. Lane looked up, surprise on his face, and stood up.

"I'm not sure what happened. But I needed to know that you were okay." He took a hesitant step toward me but stopped. He looked sad in a way I had never seen. As if I had let him down in such a way that had never happened to him before. I was screwing up more than just myself here.

I sat down on the couch, silent. I could hardly think right now.

Lane sat down next to me, but not too closely, as if he wasn't sure I would want him closer. I did, God knows I did, but at the same time I couldn't bear anybody close to me right now.

"I don't know where to start. And until I can figure that out, I can't really talk about it." I couldn't even look at Lane while I spoke.

How do I explain to him that I'm hearing voices? Seeing things nobody else can see? Having dreams that make me feel like I know nothing about my life?

I felt Lane take my hand gently. "Abby. I don't need to know. Not if you're not ready to tell. I'm just here for you. However you need me to be."

Feeling tears in my eyes again, I took a shaky breath, inhaling deeply. "Thank you. That's more than I could ask for."

I would tell him. Eventually. Okay, maybe not. I couldn't bear to have him disappear on me. Even with knowing Lane only a short time, he seemed to have become a fixture in my life. Having a constant in my life had become a lifeline for me.

We just sat there in silence for a while, Lane holding my hand. I had calmed down and wasn't crying anymore.

"I don't know about you two, but I could use a drink!" Whitney said, barging into the living room.

I laughed. "Whitney, it's barely noon."

"Hey," she said, "if it's after noon, then it's okay for a drink! What do you say, Lane? You down? Your brother can join too, if he wants."

Lane looked at me, as if asking for permission. I smiled at him. I didn't care what we did, but I didn't want Lane to leave yet.

He smiled back and nodded at Whitney. "I'll go call him." He got up and went to the kitchen.

Whitney came and sat down. "Are you okay? I hope you're not mad about him being here. He looked so distraught but wouldn't tell me what happened."

I looked to the kitchen to make sure Lane couldn't hear us. Turning back, I said softly, "I heard my mom."

Whitney leaned back. "What do you mean? Like, she called you?"

I shook my head. "No. Like I heard her. Like she was right next to me or something!"

"How's that possible?"

"I have no idea!" I hissed. "But it happened. We were just sitting there talking and suddenly I hear my mom saying, 'I love you'!"

"This is really freaking me out Abigail."

"You? How do you think I feel?"

Whitney nodded. "But you didn't tell Lane?"

I shook my head. "How can I? 'Hey, Lane, I'm hearing voices and seeing things nobody else can see.' Really? That's going to make him run for the hills!"

"Yes, that's true. Good point."

"So, for now, I'm stuck. I can't let him know. But on the other hand, I don't know how long I can keep it from him. Maybe I need to be locked away in a hospital." I sighed.

"No, no, no." Whitney rubbed my shoulder. "Don't think like that. Stay positive. There's a reason for what's going on and you going crazy is not it!"

I smiled at her. "Thank you. You've been a good friend through all of this."

"That's what I'm here for."

She leaned in for a hug. It felt really good to be held and comforted. I hadn't realized how much I had needed that until now. I felt safe and secure, two things that I had been lacking lately.

Lane cleared his throat, and we drew apart. "Kent said he's down for some day drinking and he's on his way."

Whitney smiled. "Great! I'm going to see what drinks we have in stock." She left for the kitchen.

Lane took her seat on the couch, looking at me. "I'll stay as long as you want me to."

I seized the moment to be bold. "And what if I want you around for a long time?"

Lane's mouth lifted in a half-smile and I felt my heart flutter. "What if I said that was totally fine?"

I smiled back. "I'd say that's totally fine with me too."

"Good," Lane said before leaning in to kiss me. He stopped right before our lips met, meeting my eyes to make sure it was okay. I felt our breath mingle and he was *so close* to me and I couldn't stand it anymore. The side of his mouth curved up in a smile before leaning in the rest of the way.

My breath hitched, and I felt my heart speed up. I laced my hands through his hair, holding him to me. I scooted closer, pulling Lane toward me as I did. I felt breathless but never more alive.

Lane moved one hand to the back of my neck, holding me in place. He trailed kisses down the side of my neck, causing me to shiver. He came back to my mouth, claiming it as his.

I leaned in closer, my whole body on fire. Lane put his hands on my shoulders, slowing us down. He kissed me again, softly, before pulling back. His eyes were bright, his breathing heavy.

I stared at him, winded. "Wow," I whispered.

Lane grinned. "Definitely a wow."

I smiled back. I felt like I could kiss Lane forever. I didn't care who saw or what they thought.

I started to lean back in before I caught myself. It was so easy to forget my problems when I was with Lane, but I had to be careful. I couldn't allow myself to get carried away, not with my problems.

Sitting back, I moved away from Lane. I noticed him frowning and said quickly, "I'm sure Whitney is about to come back."

Lane looked at me but then nodded. "Sure. I wouldn't want to make her uncomfortable."

I swallowed and looked around, trying to save the situation. "So, any luck on the job front yet?"

"Job? Oh, no, not yet. Kent and I are just gambling with the fact of trying to find jobs before we run out of money."

I frowned. *Why did that sound so familiar?* Suddenly, I flashed back to the night I met Kent and Lane at the bar. Kent had said the exact same thing to me then. *That's really weird.*

"Oh, really? What kind of work are you hoping to get in to?"

Lane shrugged. "Well, I used to manage a few stores back home. I guess I was hoping to get into something similar here."

"Well, you can always use me as a reference if you need to."

Lane smiled. "Well, thanks."

Whitney chose that moment to pop back in with Kent. "Look who showed up on our doorstep! The poor thing looked lost, so I let him in." She playfully patted Kent on the cheek.

Kent stepped back. "Okay, ha, ha. I heard there was going to be some drinking, so I decided to stop by. Gotta be responsible for my brother and all that."

Lane laughed. "Says the guy who climbed into a fountain on a drunken dare! Naked, I might add!"

Kent's cheeks turned red while we laughed. Whitney, I had noticed, seemed to be paying more attention now.

"Yeah, well, at least I didn't striptease for the whole bar that night!"

It was my turn to look more interested now. "Striptease? Well, give it a few shots, I may need to see this!"

Lane's face turned red. "Let's not repeat that experience. Nobody needs to see that."

Whitney winked at me. "Oh, I can think of someone who needs to see it."

"Oh, God, Whitney," I said, covering my face with my hands.

I made my way to the kitchen, where Whitney had set up our entire liquor collection. "Okay, we're definitely set. We just need food now."

"No problem! I've got pizza on the way."

"Yes! Thank you so much for that. I'm actually pretty hungry."

"No sweat. I only ask one thing. Please try to forget about what's going on for a while? I think it'll do you good."

"I think so too, so I'm going to try. No weirdness from me, I promise." I held up my hand in a Girl Scout salute.

I knew I needed a day off from thinking about things. They were to the point of overwhelming me, almost driving me crazy. I couldn't allow myself to get there. I had to stay grounded and go with what I knew was real.

A while later, we were eating pizza in the living room, exchanging our craziest drunk stories.

Whitney shook her head, laughing. "Okay, no, that is *not* what happened! I was dared to go up to one of the bachelorettes and give her a lap dance! The kiss was a freebie!"

My cheeks were hurting from laughing so much. I looked up and noticed Lane watching me, smiling. "What about you, Abby? Let's hear it."

"Oh, no, I'm a good girl who controls my alcohol intake."

Whitney snorted. "Now that's a damned lie if I ever heard one. I've got plenty of stories for you guys," she said, turning toward them.

I waved my hands at her. "Okay, okay, okay! I give in. I think my weirdest dare was licking ketchup off someone's back."

Kent grimaced. "Please tell me it was a girl's back so I'm not so grossed out."

I laughed. "It was not, unfortunately. But at least it wasn't a hairy one!"

I was having such a good time, I didn't want it to end. I hadn't felt so relaxed in a long time. I looked around at the others, my eyes lingering on Lane as he laughed at something Kent said.

Maybe everything will be okay, I thought. *It can't get worse than this.*

Chapter Four

I was in the bathroom washing the pizza grease off my hands. After drying them, I looked at myself in the mirror and frowned. *Bleh*, I thought. I looked awful. Too pale.

I put on a little bit of blush and ran some mascara over my lashes. A tiny bit of lip gloss and I was done. *I hope that's not too obvious.*

I went to open the door right as Lane was about to walk in.

"Oh, sorry!" I exclaimed.

He smiled. "I should be the one apologizing, I almost knocked you down." He took a moment to look over me, causing my face to heat up. "Looking good, Abby."

I tried to take in a breath to steady myself. "Thanks, Lane."

He reached up to tuck a strand of hair back behind my ear. "It's always my pleasure, Abby," he said gently.

Boy, did he know how to make my legs go weak. I put a hand to the doorframe to steady myself. "Uh, I should get out of your way then." I took a step forward, but Lane didn't move backward.

I was face-to-face with his chest and I could smell him, a mix of cologne and *Lane* and it just seemed *so right*. I inhaled deeply, looking up at him. He was staring down at me with a small smile.

He lifted his hands to brush my hair back, cupping my face. He leaned down, kissing one corner of my mouth, and then the other corner, before finally reaching the center of my lips where I wanted him most.

As he did, I gasped, not used to the flames coursing through me as Lane kissed me again. I pulled him toward me, crushing any space that was left between us.

Lane pushed me back against the doorframe, tugging on my hair to bring my face up to him. He seemed as out of breath as I was. His hands ran down my arms, up my back, over my hips, and I just couldn't keep it straight anymore.

His mouth was moving away from mine, and I turned my head, wanting it back. But then he was trailing his kisses down my neck, on my collarbone – *and I felt like my bones were melting* – to the other side of my neck. Back to my mouth. His lips parted mine and I sighed, never wanting this moment to end.

But too soon it did, Lane pulling back slowly, giving me time to find my feet again. I was breathing so hard it was embarrassing. Except I couldn't find it in me to care.

I leaned my forehead on his chest. "What are you doing to me?" I whispered, my eyes shut.

I felt more than heard Lane's laugh. "I could ask you the same." He kissed the top of my head and stepped back.

I looked at him. Of course, he didn't seem affected by that earth-shattering moment at all. Whereas I felt like I had been run over by a truck. In the only good way that could feel.

"Okay," I said, smoothing down my shirt, "now I should really get back out there."

Lane smiled down at me. "Yes, sure. I'll be right there soon." He stepped into the bathroom and shut the door.

I blew out a breath, leaning forward, hands on my knees. "Wow," I said. I was convinced. There was never going to be anyone else who could do to me what Lane does.

I went to the living room and sat down. I picked up my beer and looked up. Whitney and Kent were just sitting and staring. Kent snorted and looked away while Whitney raised her eyebrows at me with a knowing smile.

"What?" I asked, feeling exposed, like they knew what had just happened.

Whitney cleared her throat and patted down her hair, widening her eyes at me. I just stared at her, confused. She patted her head again, and I realized she meant for me to copy her. I reached up and felt the bird's nest that was supposed to be my hair. My cheeks burned as I fixed the mess Lane's hands had left up there. Whitney was grinning at me and I narrowed my eyes at her.

"Shut up," I muttered at them.

"We didn't say anything," Whitney said, grinning at me.

I glared at her anyways. This was humiliating. Like a walk of shame humiliating.

Lane chose that moment to come back out, sitting down by me. He looked at each of us before asking, "Okay, what did I miss?"

Whitney grinned. "Oh, it doesn't look like you missed anything."

"Oh my God, Whitney," I whispered, covering my face with my hands. "You're the worst."

Whitney laughed. "Oh, come on! I'm just teasing! It was too easy."

I looked at Lane, who was actually blushing now. It made me feel a little better to know he could be affected, too.

Lane stood up. "Okay. Enough fun at our expense." He turned to me. "Want to get out of here?"

I nodded. "Definitely." I stood up and got my purse from my room.

Whitney gave me a little wave as we left, and I shook my head at her. She always knew just what buttons to push.

After getting into Lane's car, he looked over and asked, "Now what? Do you want to grab some dinner?"

I shook my head. "No, I'm not really hungry right now." I looked around outside. "How about we go to the park?"

Lane shrugged. "Sure. Sounds good." He turned the car and started driving.

I let my mind wander as I watched our surroundings flash by. This had been a really great day for me. *Okay, minus the freak out this morning.* It made me realize how great my friends were. Even though Whitney was the only one who knew my secret. Which made me feel kind of guilty for not telling Lane. I just didn't know how to tell without scaring him off. I needed him.

As if he could sense my tumultuous thoughts, Lane glanced at me and reached for my hand to hold. He brought it to his lips, brushing them over my knuckles.

I blushed again, wondering if *that* reaction was ever going to get under control.

"We're here," Lane said, pulling into a parking spot.

I got out, looking around. There were a few walking trails with benches spaced out. I saw families out on the playground watching their kids race around the equipment, tagging each other before turning and dashing away.

The sun was still high in the sky, with only a few clouds for cover from its heat. I swatted away some flies as I went to the front of the car where Lane waited for me.

"Lead the way," he said, gesturing to the paths that disappeared into the trees.

I smiled at him and started walking. As I did, I felt Lane move up beside me. Moving into the shade, I felt calmer than I had in days.

"You know, I always loved this place as a kid," I said. "I could be whatever I wanted on that playground. A pirate on a ship, a princess locked in a tower. It was all so simple back then. Find the treasure, rescue the girl. And then it was over."

Lane looked down at me. "And now what? Are you still in need of rescue?"

I glanced down at the sidewalk we were following. "Maybe. I thought I was okay. Everything was great. And then I realized it might not be that simple."

"I bet it could be that simple. You've got people around you that care about you and want to help you." Lane took up my hand and laced our fingers together, holding me tightly. "I'm here, too. And I care about you."

He stopped walking and pulled me to him. "Do you trust me? That I would never hurt you?"

I nodded at him. "I do. But I'm afraid of you leaving me, too."

Lane's face softened, and he stroked my cheek with his free hand. "I couldn't leave you even if I wanted to. Which I don't, by the way," he added hastily.

I laughed and wiped at my eyes, where tears were threatening to fall. "You might. I couldn't be selfish enough to ask you to stay once you know everything."

It was time. Time to face my fears head on. I couldn't keep running away. That wasn't who I was. I wasn't a coward.

I steered us to a bench that was set back in a canopy of trees. I sat down and Lane followed.

I looked straight ahead as I spoke, worried to see how he would react. "It's hard to speak of. It sounds insane. And I'll understand if it's too much for you to handle."

I took a deep breath, my fingers fidgeting together. "I saw something in the manuscript I'm currently reading for work. Something impossible. Because nobody else can see it."

Lane stiffened up but didn't say anything.

"It was a note," I continued, "saying I've been in a coma for five years and I needed to wake up. I showed it to my boss and to Whitney and neither of them can see it. And then I've been having strange dreams that make me wonder if it could be true. Hearing things that make me feel like I'm going crazy. Because nobody else can see or hear them."

I looked at Lane in desperation. "Do you understand now? Why I ran away this morning? I heard my mom's voice clear as day as if she was right next to me. There's something wrong with me and I don't know how to fix it." My voice started cracking as I broke down crying.

Lane looked down at me before wrapping me in his arms and drawing me close. I laid my head on his chest and cried out all the anxiety, the hopelessness of my situation.

After a few minutes, I started to breathe easier. I sat back and wiped at my eyes and nose. I couldn't bring myself to look at Lane.

"Are you feeling better now?" he asked softly, brushing his hand over my hair, smoothing it down.

Nodding, I realized I truly did feel better. A weight was gone that I hadn't fully noticed was pushing me down. I felt lighter just telling someone about my secret.

I took a shaky breath. "Now is the part where you tell me you can't see me anymore and I need help."

Lane chuckled and took hold of my hand again. "I'm not leaving you Abby. In fact, I'd like to look at the note."

I froze, looking at him. "You're really not leaving?" I whispered, surprised.

"I'm not leaving," he whispered back. "I can't say I understand what you're going through, but I want to help you."

I could only sit there, stunned. This guy was too much. I didn't deserve him. Shaking my head, I stood up. "No, no this is too much." I started walking. "I can't drag you into this with me."

Lane jumped up and ran in front of me, blocking my way. "Wait, Abby, where are you going?"

I wiped at my eyes again, tears flooding over. "I'm leaving. I *am* insane. No guy in their right mind would willingly stay with me after that. So, I must be going out of my mind. I've made you up, you're a figment of my imagination."

Lane just stared at me, biting back a smile. "Abby, look at me."

I sighed, reluctantly bringing my eyes up to meet his. Lane was looking at me, and I was amazed to see no skepticism in his expression. He wasn't making fun of me or indulging me.

He took hold of my hand, bringing it to his cheek to touch. "Do I feel like a figment of your imagination?"

I shook my head, unable to speak.

He took a step closer, so there was no space left between us. He wrapped his arms around me. "Does this feel real to you?"

I clung to Lane, needing to feel grounded, to feel real. "Yes," I whispered. "You feel real." I hugged him tighter to me.

"Okay, then," Lane said, kissing the top of my head. He led me back to the bench. Wiping my tears away, he smiled at me. "Whenever you're ready, I'm here for you."

I nodded, drawing in a shaky breath. I smoothed my hair back and wiped my face off.

"God, this is going horribly," I said. I reached over to my purse, digging through the contents until I grabbed onto the page that had turned my life upside down. I handed it to Lane, watching as he read it.

He bent his head over the page, and I noticed how he mouthed the words sometimes as he read them. It got harder to breathe as he got closer to where I knew the note to be. He read past it and kept going. I let out the breath I hadn't noticed I was holding.

I sat back and looked up at the sky through the trees. I was truly alone. Nobody could help me.

"Abby?"

I didn't move. "Yeah?"

"Nobody else can see the note?"

"No," I breathed out, close to breaking down again, tears squeezing out of the corners of my eyes.

"Abby?"

"Yeah?"

I felt Lane take my hand. "I can see it."

The whole world shifted on its axis, causing me to lose my breath. I clutched Lane's hand like a life preserver, saving me from floating away.

"You can?" I turned to look at him. "You really can, you're not just saying that?"

Lane pulled the paper up so I could see it and he pointed out the exact spot where the note started. "It's there, isn't it? It says it's a new technology, they don't know how you'll receive the message."

All I could do was stare at him. "You're not messing with me, are you?" I asked, too afraid to be let down again.

Lane shook his head no. "Please, believe me. I would never hurt you like that. I swear I can see what you're talking about."

"You can see it? You can really see it? So, I'm not going crazy?" I didn't even know how to react. "But wait! *How* can you see it? Whitney and my boss couldn't, how can you?"

Lane shrugged. "I honestly don't know. But I see it, just like you can."

I rubbed my face with my hands. "Okay, so what does this even mean? Are you part of my delusion or is this all a big joke?"

"This is no delusion. You're perfectly fine and you're going to keep being fine."

"Well, now what? How does this help me? This still doesn't make any sense!" I slumped back against the bench, feeling despair steal over me.

Lane rubbed my shoulders. "It's okay. This can be a good starting point for you."

I threw up my hands. "Yeah, but how? What am I going to do, go around and show everybody this paper to see if they can see it or not? I don't think so," I said, shaking my head.

Lane laughed. "Yes, that's true, but that's also not what I had in mind. I think your idea would take just a little too long with no results."

My cheeks flamed up at the teasing tone of his voice. I sat up straighter, crossing my arms. "Okay, then mister smarty-pants, what was your idea?"

Lane smiled and stood up. "As much as I'm loving seeing this feisty side of you, sitting here and arguing isn't going to get us anywhere." He extended his hand to me, to help me stand up.

I pushed it away and got up on my own. "I'm not arguing, you're arguing," I said, as I started walking back down the pathway. I didn't bother waiting for Lane to catch up.

I didn't need to worry though, because he caught up with me easily enough.

"Not arguing, huh?" he asked easily.

"Nope," I said flatly, not looking at him.

"Okay. Just making sure."

I dared to look at him out of the corner of my eye and saw him grinning down at me. I huffed and turned away, walking faster.

Lane kept pace with me and I felt his arm go around my shoulders, hugging me to him. My heartbeat picked up. I just couldn't resist this man.

I slowed down a bit to a normal walking pace and leaned into Lane a little. He responded by squeezing me to him, kissing the top of my head.

I sighed. "Okay, fine, I overreacted. So where are we going?"

"Back to your place," Lane responded. "I figured Whitney could help us out since she's already in the loop."

Ugh. Back to Whitney's teasing and innuendos. I didn't think I could stomach much more of it. But I knew I would have to, for my sake.

"Okay. Back to my place. To figure out…something."

Lane nodded. "It's going to be okay Abby. I won't let anything happen to you."

I ducked my head, feeling heat rising in my cheeks. I still couldn't believe I had lucked out with such an amazing man. Wrapping my arm around his waist, I squeezed him back, feeling the firm muscles of his stomach. My whole face felt like it was on fire now.

"How about we pick up some dinner on the way back?" Lane asked.

We had reached the car by then and I paused by the passenger door. "I could definitely go for some Chinese food right now."

"Chinese it is then!" Lane said enthusiastically.

We both got in our seats and Lane pulled out onto the street.

"I'll text Whitney and see what she wants," I said. I pulled my phone out and opened it to our conversation.

Me: *Hey, Whit, we're going to bring home some Chinese for dinner. You want anything?*

Whitney: *Yeah, I want to know what happened with you guys! You ran out of here pretty fast!*

I rolled my eyes at that.

Me: *I wonder why! You and your stupid sex jokes*

Whitney: *Lol, you know I was just teasing! Seriously though, where did you guys go?*

Me: *To the park to talk.* I wasn't sure how much I should tell her over a text message. *It's a bit of a long story. I was going to fill you in when we got back*

Whitney: *Okay, fine. And I'll take beef and broccoli with an eggroll*

Me: *Got it! See you soon*

Whitney: *Don't forget the sweet and sour sauce!*

Me: *Okay, mom*

I put my phone down. "Okay, I have Whitney's order."

"Good. I'll run in and order if you'll tell me what you want."

Lane was pulling into the parking lot of Chef Noodle. It was moderately busy; the parking spots were half full.

"Will you get me orange chicken and some of the rangoons? Oh, and Whitney wants beef and broccoli and an eggroll."

"Got it. I'll be right back."

Lane leaned in toward me slowly, eyes playing over my face. I could feel every glance like a soft caress and then I was leaning in too. His lips pressed softly against mine, and now I've forgotten how to breathe. Too soon, the moment ended and Lane moved away, smiling.

"That's never going to get old."

I blushed again, biting my lip. Anything with Lane would never get old. I watched as he got out and I leaned my head back against the seat, my breath whooshing out.

I observed the other customers going in and out, noticing that nobody glanced in my direction. It would ordinarily have never bothered me, but after the day I had, I needed the normalcy of random people walking around and glancing in my direction, even for a second.

I sat forward, being as obvious as I could about watching the people walk by. And yet nobody would turn my way.

Oh, please let this all be in my head, I thought, feeling desperation come over me.

My mouth had dried out and my palms were getting sweaty. I didn't want to start panicking for no reason, but I almost couldn't stop myself. I was alone in the world, nobody could see me.

Without thinking it through, I reached over to the steering wheel and pressed down on the horn. If I couldn't get people to see me, then I would force them to see me now. I had to do it, I had to reassure myself I was really here, that I was in this world. There was a haze over my vision, a fog over my thoughts. I couldn't stop myself, couldn't take my hand off the horn.

"Abby? Abby, what are you doing?"

Lane was in the driver's seat, prying my hands from the wheel, letting the horn finally fall silent.

I didn't say anything. I didn't think I could say anything. All I could do was stare at the steering wheel, breathing hard.

Lane lifted my face gently with his hand, bringing it up to meet his gaze. His brow was furrowed with concern. "What happened, Abby?"

"I don't know," I whispered, my thoughts still felt muddled. "I wanted the other people to see me. I needed to make sure I was real."

Lane's thumb grazed over my cheek, back and forth. "Okay. Let's get you home, okay?"

I nodded numbly. I could feel myself falling apart, but I couldn't figure out how to stop it. I looked down at my hands. They wouldn't stop shaking.

Lane moved the food he had set down on his seat to the back and climbed in, starting the car. He glanced at me and took my hand in his, rubbing it gently. "We'll be home soon."

I nodded and looked out the window, not paying attention to our surroundings. No time at all had passed before Lane stopped the car. We were back at the apartment.

Lane grabbed the food and we made our way upstairs. I unlocked the door and saw Whitney waiting for us in the kitchen. She looked up as we approached, a smile on her face to greet us. It quickly fell into a look of confusion as she looked back and forth between the two of us.

I could only imagine what she was seeing. Lane, hovering protectively over me, guiding me into the room. I hadn't quite come out of my funk yet. I felt slightly robotic, letting Lane put me where I needed to be. My face felt stiff, like I couldn't use my muscles anymore. I was going off the deep end, unable to care anymore. So what if I wasn't real? Why should I care? I shouldn't. I was just a figment of someone's imagination, a person in someone's dream. It was the only explanation. Right?

Whitney rushed over, hands clasping my shoulders, looking me over. "What happened? Is she okay?"

Lane nodded. "I think she'll be okay in a few. She kind of had a breakdown at the Chinese place. She said nobody could see her; she wanted to make sure she was real."

Whitney inhaled sharply, hand covering her mouth. "Abigail, can you hear me? Are you okay?"

I nodded. "I'm fine. It's all fine. Perfectly fine."

Whitney just stared at me. Then she drew herself up, an angry look on her face. "Abigail, you listen to me! You will snap out of this, *now*!" She grabbed me by the arms and shook me. "You are not allowed to lose yourself, not now! Get it together!" She looked at me with tears in her eyes.

I looked at her, finally focusing my gaze. I saw the panic on her face and felt a twinge deep in my belly. I had caused this. I glanced at Lane, noticing a similar expression on his face.

I drew in a shaky breath, trying to keep my face from crumpling under the tears trying to drown me. "I'm sorry," I whispered. "I don't know what happened. I can't believe I did that." I looked back and forth between the two of them. "I'm sorry."

Lane closed the distance between us, wrapping me into him, holding me close. "It's okay, you're okay." He drew back, looking at me. "You scared me though, Abby."

"Me too," Whitney chimed in. She hugged me close. "Please stay with us. You're too important to us."

Hot tears pricked at my eyes, threatening to fall. I could feel my face wanting to scrunch up, but I pulled myself together. Now was not the time. "I'm okay now. Thank you, guys." I shook my head, wiping my face off and taking a deep breath. "Now, who's eating?"

"I'll get the plates," Whitney said, moving the food boxes to the kitchen table, leaving me and Lane alone.

I turned to him, feeling more than a little embarrassed. I couldn't even meet his eyes.

He solved that problem, tilting my face up to meet his. He didn't seem completely satisfied. "You scared me," he said softly.

I hugged him to me, burying my head into his chest. "I'm so sorry. I'm scaring myself. I let everything overwhelm me and I...I don't know." I leaned back to look at him. "I'm sorry."

Lane smiled. "It's okay. Just stay with me, okay?"

I nodded. "I will."

"Dinner's ready!" Whitney yelled from the dining room.

I grabbed Lane's hand, lacing our fingers together. We headed to the table, and my mouth started watering at the smells. Sweet, spicy, sour, garlic. I couldn't wait to eat.

We all sat down at our plates that Whitney had already made. I took a deep breath, sniffing the chicken and rice on my plate. It was helping to bring me back to reality.

After filling up on everything, I leaned back, contemplating unbuttoning my pants. *Yeah, like that would be attractive*, I snorted to myself.

"Okay, I think we need to focus again," Lane stated, pushing his plate away from him. He motioned to Whitney. "You know what I'm talking about?"

Whitney nodded at that.

"Okay," Lane continued, "Well when we went to the park today, Abby filled me in on the note. Nobody else can see it."

"Right," Whitney agreed.

"Well, Abby showed it to me. I can see it."

There was dead silence as Whitney processed this information.

Then, "What!"

"He can see it, Whitney," I reassured her. "We have no idea what it means."

Whitney just sat there, gaping at us. "Are you serious? What does this even mean? I mean…what?"

I shook my head. "I showed it to him, he pointed out exactly where it was and read it back to me."

Whitney sat back. "My mind is blown right now. Let me see it again. Maybe I'll be able to see it now, too."

I got up from the table and walked to my purse, grabbing the page from inside. I nervously unfolded it, trying to flatten out the creases in it. I sat back down and handed it to Whitney.

She leaned over the page, eyes roaming back and forth as she read it over again. I glanced at Lane, and he reached over to grab my hand.

"Damn it!" Whitney said, frustrated. "It's still not there! Why can *he* see it then?"

"It doesn't make sense," I repeated. I looked over at Lane for help.

"I'm still not a delusion, if that's what you're implying," he said.

"But, why? Why, why, why?" I said, starting to get angry at all of this.

"Okay, how about we put that on the back burner for now?" Whitney suggested. "What's the plan now?"

"Maybe we really digest the note. We can maybe make sense of it," Lane replied.

I nodded. "Let me write out some copies, so you each have one."

A few minutes later, we each had a copy of the note in front of us. Whitney paled a little as she read it fully for the first time.

"Okay," she started, "so for the sake of argument, maybe we make a list of why this note could be true."

Lane and I both looked at her, incredulous. "Really?" I asked. "How will that help?"

Whitney shrugged. "I'm not sure. But what have we got to lose?"

I just stared at her. "Okay, fine. So, let's see. Five years ago. I told you that's when my migraines started."

Whitney jumped up. "Hold that thought. Let me grab something to write this all down."

I looked over at Lane. "This is insane. I can't possibly be in a coma, dreaming all of this up!"

Lane nodded. "I agree. But let's take it one step at a time."

Whitney returned and sat down. "Okay. One: migraines started." She looked at me. "You're sure you don't remember how they started?"

I shook my head. "No. But it's always in the same spot." I touched the left side of my head.

"Okay. What else?"

I shrugged, trying to think. "Hearing voices? Having crazy dreams?"

Whitney was nodding as she wrote that down.

"I don't think this is really anything, but…" I trailed off.

"Hey, anything could help," Whitney reassured me.

"I can't ever get my mom on the phone," I said. "I honestly can't remember the last time we spoke."

Whitney added it to the list. "Who knows, it could be important."

"I can't think of anything else. And I'm really tired." I rubbed my eyes, feeling exhaustion steal over me.

"Sure, let's call it a night." Whitney got up to start cleaning.

Lane stood up and helped me out of my chair. He pulled me in for a hug. "I guess I'll get going."

"Thanks for everything today, Lane. I'm glad I didn't scare you off. I know this is all really crazy."

"Hey, I meant what I said. I want to be here for you and help you."

I smiled into his shirt. "I love hearing that."

"I love saying it." He pressed a kiss onto my head. "I'll see you later, okay?"

"Okay." I walked with him to the door. "See you later."

I leaned my head on the door after it closed behind him. "I am so over today," I mumbled to myself.

I went to my room, managing to get some pajamas on before I crashed onto my bed, falling asleep just as quickly.

Chapter Five

I woke up the next morning feeling more refreshed than I had in a while. There was a new energy coursing through me. It made me feel buoyant and hopeful.

I lied in bed with my eyes closed, smiling to myself. The sun peeking into my window warmed my face. *Today will be a good day*, I told myself. I could use a little pat on the back to encourage me to keep going.

These last few days had scared the hell out of me. I could feel myself spiraling out of control. Thankfully, I had two amazing lifelines that always made sure to keep me grounded. Minus a few bumps,

Whitney had been by my side since the day I had met her.

It was during my Junior year of college and my roommate, Kristi, had just informed me she was moving in with her boyfriend.

"What?" I shrieked, waving my hands at her. "You can't just move out, we signed a year-long lease! We still have seven months left!"

Kristi shrugged. "Sorry. Mike said this was our last chance to work things out."

I could feel my eyes bugging out of my head. "Are you kidding me? How am I supposed to afford rent now?"

"Beats me," Kristi said, grabbing her suitcase out of the closet. "But it's your name on the lease, not mine, remember? I was late to the lease signing and you said it was okay if just your name was on it, as long as I paid my half. Well, now I'm done paying my half and I'm moving out. I'm going to make it work with Mike; I need to make it work this time. It's not my problem."

I clenched my hands, forcing them to stay at my sides so that I didn't pummel her and go to jail. Instead, I went to my laptop and sat down with it. I made up a flier seeking a new roommate and printed out a bunch of copies.

Grabbing my purse, I took the fliers and started leaving them wherever I could. The apartment lobby, the café where I got my coffee every morning, the student union on campus. I was desperate. There was no way I could keep the apartment on my own.

It took two days before I started getting calls. Even though I had specified that I was looking for a female roommate, I was surprised at the amount of men who called.

On the fifth day, I was feeling defeated. I was looking online at other apartments for when I got kicked out.

My phone rang, distracting me out of my misery. "Hello?"

"Hi, is this Abigail?"

I sighed. "Yes, it is."

"Hi! My name is Whitney! I'm calling about the roommate ad you put out."

This girl had some high energy. *It's worth a shot*, I considered. "Yeah, why don't I meet you later to discuss the details?"

"Sure! Can't wait!" Whitney exclaimed.

We had met and clicked immediately. We were soul sisters. Now we had been living together for the past five years.

My other lifeline, Lane, well he had come along just when I needed him. He was definitely a rock to lean on, a pair of arms to hold me up.

Strong, muscly arms, I thought, smiling. I couldn't seem to get enough of them. And that scared me. I had never met someone like him or been so attracted to a guy before. Was it bad to fall for someone so fast?

I shook my head and rolled over, shoving my head under my pillow. No, I wasn't falling for him. Not yet, anyway. Lane was someone I could see myself with for a long time though. Maybe once all this nonsense had settled down, we could really focus on just being together. Not Lane having to pick me up every time I was down. I didn't want to be someone he was always rescuing.

"I'm not a damsel!" I growled, sitting up.

I could feel myself getting angry. "Not today," I said. "Today will be a good day. No weirdness, no freaking out." Taking a deep breath, I stood up to get dressed.

Music was playing from the stereo in the living room and I saw Whitney dancing around in the kitchen while she cooked. I smiled as I took a seat at the bar.

Whitney turned around, smiling when she saw me. "Good morning!" she sang as she pushed bacon and fried eggs in my direction.

"Good morning yourself," I said, scooping up my portion onto my plate. "You seem pretty chipper this morning."

"That's because I am!" she replied, sitting beside me to make her plate. "This new guy started at work the other day. Super cute. He texted me last night."

I raised my eyebrows. "Oh yeah? What's going on there?"

Whitney grinned at me before taking a drink of coffee. "No clue yet. But I think he'll be fun to play with."

I snorted and covered my mouth as I giggled.

"I'll see him at work soon, so that'll be fun," she added.

I nodded. "Yeah, good luck with your new endeavor."

Whitney made a face and stuck her tongue out at me. "Oh, whatever. I need a distraction. Plus, I don't want to live vicariously through you and your relationship."

My cheeks burned as embarrassment shot through me. "It's not a relationship! We haven't even talked about that."

Whitney smirked at me. "Oh, so you're just hooking up with Lane for fun?"

Now my whole face was on fire. "We are not!" I replied indignantly. "There is zero hooking up going on."

Whitney just raised her eyebrows at me.

"Just kissing," I gave in. "Amazing, earth-shattering kissing."

"Earth-shattering, huh?" Whitney asked. "Now I'm jealous. He's hot and a great kisser? I seriously need a boyfriend. Spill the details!"

"I will not!" I exclaimed.

"Oh, come on!" Whitney begged. "For your best friend?" She started giving me puppy dog eyes.

I narrowed my eyes at her. "Okay, fine. You're incorrigible. When we kiss it makes me feel like we're the only two people on earth. All of his attention is on me. And his lips," I sighed, "they're so soft, yet it's like they convey all his feelings in a kiss. Not to mention he's incredibly well-built. Like a solid wall of muscles."

I turned back to Whitney to find her gaping at me. "What?"

"Nothing! I mean, wow. That sounds incredible. I can't wait to hear how he is in bed."

I choked on a bite of my eggs. "Oh my God, no Whitney. Besides, it might not even come to that! I don't sleep with just anyone, you know."

"I know, I'm sorry," Whitney said, covering my hand with hers. "I am happy for you, really. It's just easy to tease you sometimes."

I rolled my eyes. "Thanks. Now you'll get no more details about me and Lane."

"Spoilsport," she muttered.

"Nosy Nellie," I retorted.

****

As the day went on, I started feeling like my old self again. I wasn't having any weird feelings. It was turning out to be a regular boring day. I loved it.

Whitney had texted me a few times, sending what looked like covert pictures of her new boy-toy co-worker. All of her pictures were at an angle, either of the side of his face or it was blurry, like she was putting the phone down before she could be found out that she was taking his picture. From what I could tell, he was definitely easy on the eyes.

I texted her back before settling down on the couch, cocooning myself in the blankets we always had laid out.

"Just a short nap," I told myself before drifting off.

I woke up later to the sound of my phone's notifications. The sun had moved around the apartment, now slanting across the hallway wall, slowly climbing its way up.

I sat up and stretched, moving the blankets away from me. I grabbed my phone. There were a couple of texts from Whitney, but I felt myself getting excited when I saw one from Lane.

Lane: *Just checking on you. Been thinking about you today ;-)*

He had even sent a winking smiley face. I would have laughed if I hadn't found it so adorable.

Me: *I'm good. Just having a lazy day. Finally!*

It wasn't long before I heard my text tone go off.

Lane: *Oh yeah? Sleeping the day away?*

My cheeks burned as I glanced back at my impromptu bed. *Whatever*, I thought, *it was a short nap anyway.*

Me: *No, I wasn't. Just relaxing, enjoying having the apartment to myself*

Lane: *Alone, huh?*

I pressed my lips together to keep from grinning.

Me: *Yep. All alone*

Lane: *Want some company?*

Me: *I would, but Whitney should be home soon. She can keep me company ;-)*

Lane: *You're killing me here*

Me: *Sorry. I'll see you soon though*

Lane: *I can't wait*

I set the phone down before I could write back. Better to leave him hanging. I wasn't about to be the clingy girl.

Going to the kitchen, I started getting dinner ready. Fried chicken, one of Whitney's favorites and one I could actually cook pretty well.

As the oil was sputtering in the pan, I laid a few pieces of flour-covered chicken in to cook. I had just put in the last piece when I heard the front door open and close, with Whitney calling out a greeting.

"In the kitchen!" I yelled out, wiping my hands off on a towel.

"Oh my gosh, that smells so good! I'm starving!" Whitney said.

"Good! That's what I was going for."

Whitney smiled, pouring herself a glass of wine and getting out a beer for me.

"Thanks," I said, taking it from her.

"Need any help?"

"No, I think I've got it. I'm about to mash up some potatoes and we should be set."

"Well how about I make a salad?"

"Sounds great!"

We moved around each other comfortably, dancing a routine five years in the making.

After dinner, we sat at the table, neither of us wanting to move.

"So. Stuffed," Whitney said, rubbing her stomach. "I swear you make that better than my mom." She looked up at me, pointing her finger. "Don't you tell her I said that."

I laughed. "No worries there. She scares me sometimes."

We sat there for a while, comfortable in our silence. I loved that about Whitney. There was never a need to fill the empty space, no awkward silences. We could just hang out together and not say a word.

Eventually I hefted myself up from the table, gathering our dishes as I did. Whitney followed behind, throwing away trash.

I stood at the sink, rinsing off the plates. "So, I haven't had any episodes today," I said, careful to keep my tone neutral.

"Oh, really?" Whitney replied. "I'm so glad. I was wondering, but didn't want to intrude, but then

I figured you would have told me if you'd had something happen. Especially since…well, you know, how you were with the last few."

I glanced up to see Whitney's cheeks turning red.

"I'm sorry, that came out badly," she said, running a hand through her hair.

"No, it's okay. I went a little crazy. I get it." I turned back to the sink. "Hopefully I don't do that next time."

"Oh no, there isn't going to *be* a next time!" Whitney said forcefully, placing a hand on my shoulder. "There's nothing wrong with you and you're not going to get any more episodes!"

I sniffed, sudden tears pricking at my eyes. I shook my hands off and turned, hugging Whitney hard.

"Thank you," I whispered. "I'm so happy I have you."

Whitney's hand rubbed my back. "You'll always have me. I'm not going anywhere."

We separated, smiling at each other before turning to our individual tasks again.

Later that night, I reviewed how my day had gone. I hadn't had any weird dreams, no flashbacks or hallucinations, nothing. Maybe it was finally over. I smiled at the thought as I let sleep take over me.

****

As the days passed into weeks, I was able to relax even more, getting back into my regular routine of working and being at home.

Except now I was able to add Lane into it. We were connecting on a level I had never experienced before. Sometimes I would catch him looking at me, and whenever I caught him, he would give me a wink and smile. It made my stomach flip when he looked at me like that. I don't think I had ever been happier.

I should have known it wouldn't last.

I was keeping count in my head. A little over three weeks had passed since I had freaked out at the Chinese restaurant. More than three weeks of getting back to myself, feeling a little better each day.

Being back at work helped. My boss never did bring up our meeting back when I had first seen the note.

I sat back and stretched, noticing the hour for the first time in a while.

"Hey Julie, you want to go grab some lunch?" I asked her.

She swiveled around in her chair, a smile on her face. "Sure! Just let me finish up here."

I nodded and stood up, grabbing my purse. Marking the spot on my manuscript where I had left off, I went over to Julie's desk. "Ready?"

She nodded, getting her purse out of her drawer. "Ready! Where do you want to go?"

"How about the coffee shop around the corner? They have amazing sandwiches and salad. Plus, I could use a pick-me-up."

"Perfect. Let's go."

We headed to the elevator, chatting about our current projects. Once we arrived at the coffee shop and placed our orders, we found a corner table to sit at.

Julie immediately launched into a story about her latest date. "So, Dave picked me up, and he took me to a hole-in-the-wall bar. Like, what? It was so gross, Abigail. You would not believe it. And then he tried to make a pass at me."

I nodded, thinking how lucky I was to have Lane. We may have met at a bar – okay, outside of the bar – but he had never been a creep.

When Julie's order number was called, I pulled out my phone to check for messages. There was a text from Whitney, a selfie with the hottie co-worker in the background. I snorted, shaking my head. *The lengths that girl goes to*, I laughed to myself.

I hadn't noticed that Julie had come back while I was replying to Whitney – *Yeah, real discreet there!* – so at first, I didn't realize she was talking to me.

"Wake up!"

I looked up, startled, wondering why she was being so rude. She gestured to the counter and said, "Wake up!"

Dread turned my blood to ice. I was frozen to my chair, unable to move. My breathing became shallow as I struggled for air. It was happening again, I just knew it.

I slowly turned in my seat. The man working behind the counter held a tray and was repeating those two horrifying words. He was looking around, waiting for someone to come claim the order. Waiting for me.

I glanced back at Julie, who was watching me with a confused expression. She beckoned to the counter again. "Wake up."

Taking a deep breath, I slowly stood up, praying my wooden legs would carry me to the counter. Once there, the man handed me the tray with a smile. "Wake up!" All I could do was stare at him as he walked away.

Looking around, it was obvious nobody else was hearing what I was hearing. I felt the blood drain from my face when I noticed the menu that was posted up on the wall behind the counter. Gone were the food and drink choices. Instead, every selection had been replaced with the phrase 'wake up.' I was looking at forty or so 'wake up's' glaring back at me. Mocking me.

Drawing in a shaky breath, I took a step backward, bumping into a man, causing him to drop his drink. "I'm so sorry," I said automatically.

The man looked irritated as he wiped his sleeves off. "Wake up!" he scolded loudly.

I will not break down, I will not break down, I repeated to myself as I set my tray down on someone's table and walked out of the door.

I managed to make it all the way around the corner before the tears I was keeping at bay spilled over. I covered my mouth to mask my gasping as I fought for air. After a few minutes, I was able to draw in deeper breaths, calming myself down.

I needed to get out of there, but I had no way of leaving. Julie had driven us here and I had left my things inside the restaurant with her.

Heaving myself off the wall I had been leaning against, I started walking in the direction of the office. Even if I was going crazy, I couldn't afford to just not show back up to work. It was important that I hold myself together.

Ten minutes later, I was back at work. Going to my manager's office, I let her know I was feeling sick and needed to leave. I grabbed my keys out of my desk drawer, hoping that Julie would bring my purse with her when she came back.

I reached home in record time, weaving in and out of the lunch hour traffic. Whitney wouldn't be home for a few more hours, which worked in my favor. I really needed to figure this out, and nobody else could help me, I was sure of that now.

Grabbing a beer from the fridge and a notepad and pen from a drawer, I plopped down onto the couch, ready to work.

"Okay," I muttered, "let's figure out what's wrong with Abigail."

I made a list and a timeline of everything that had happened so far. Looking at it, it scared me to realize that things seemed to be escalating. First it was the crazy dream. Now I was hallucinating things.

"Oh God." I sat up suddenly. "What if I'm sick? I probably have a brain tumor!" I slumped back and drained the rest of my beer. I was sick. Of course, that was my answer.

Resigned to my self-diagnosed illness, I drank through the rest of my six pack faster than I ever would have normally. I was lying on the couch, feeling the buzz in my head spreading out into my body until I felt fuzzy all over.

"Nobody knows what I'm going through," I told the ceiling. "Nobody can help me. I'm alone. Screw everybody else and their perfect lives."

I turned over to get off the couch and ended up falling on the floor, knocking the breath out of me. My phone's text alert sounded from the coffee table. Reaching up, I patted my hand along it until I found my phone. It was a text from Lane.

Lane: *Hey beautiful*

Me: *Well hey the re yorslef*

Lane: *Have plans tonight? I can come by for dinner*

I perked up at that. I hadn't realized how starved I was.

Me: *Okg yesbplease im so hubgry I coukd eat everything in the fiedge!!*

Lane: *Abby, what's wrong? Are you okay?*

Me: *Oh sint worry about me im fine. I've just reakize I have a brain turmo. So im dirking my worries away*

Lane didn't write back to that, so I laid my head on the floor. I needed another beer. I didn't want reality to come back to me yet. My buzz needed to stay for a while. But the ringing could stop. Yeah, that was annoying and needed to go away. I rubbed my head, hoping for it to stop. I lifted my head and realized it was my phone. Snorting at my ridiculousness, I pressed the answer button.

"'Lo?" I answered.

"Abby, are you okay? What's going on?" Lane asked.

"Lane! You would not believe the day I've had!" I said loudly, the words stumbling out of my fuzzy mouth.

"Abby, I'm on my way over. Is Whitney there?" Lane asked.

"Nope." I rolled to my back. "I'm all alone. I'm so alone."

I felt tears pricking at my eyes but blinked them back. I didn't want a pity party, I wanted to get wasted and forget my problems.

"But you know what, it's just fine!" I said, faking cheeriness. "'Cause now Whitney can't get mad when I drink all of her wine," I whispered loudly, as if I were conspiring with Lane. I started to giggle and sat up. "Actually, that's a great idea. I ran out of beer. Hey, can you bring me some more?"

Lane sighed, and I could practically see him running his hand through his hair. I stood up and stumbled to the fridge, opening it.

"Yep, Lane, bring refreshments. Whitney's wine has already been opened and won't last me long." I pulled it out of the fridge and placed it on the counter.

"Abby, I'll be there soon. How about you don't drink the wine yet so we can share it?"

I rolled my eyes and huffed. "Noooo, no way, I need this. I'm screwed, there's no fixing me, so I'm getting drunk."

"There is definitely fixing you. You can't give up on yourself. Did something happen today?"

I snorted again and attempted to roll my eyes. "You could say that." Suddenly, clarity came through my drunken haze, causing tears to spring to my eyes. "You know what Lane? Never mind about any of it. You don't need to come over. You're better off without me and my problems."

Lane's sharp intake of breath stabbed at my heart, prompting the tears to start falling. I would hate myself for this later, but I knew it was the right thing to do. Lane didn't need to be brought down by me.

"You don't want to see me anymore?"

I could hear the hurt and hesitation in Lane's voice, and I struggled to draw in a breath. My own heart felt like it was breaking.

I drew myself up straight to strengthen my resolve. "No. I don't. You can find someone better than me."

"I don't *want* someone better than you Abby. I just want you."

I sniffed, wiping the tears off my face. Drawing in a shaky breath, I said, "Well, too bad. That's what I want."

"But—"

"No," I said firmly. "I have to go. Goodbye Lane."

I put the phone down and hung up. Sobs came pouring out and I felt my heart breaking into a million tiny pieces. I sank to the floor, crying out all the anguish I had experienced lately. I cried for myself and all the suffering I was enduring. I cried for Lane and all the hurt and pain I had just caused him. My affection had started growing for him, but I carefully packaged it up in a tiny box and set it aside, not knowing now if it would have the chance to turn into love.

When my tears had dried, I got up. I was better off without dragging Lane down with me, even though it didn't feel like it. I stood up and placed the wine bottle back in the fridge. I was going out to drink.

I changed out of my work clothes and into jeans and a t-shirt, not in the mood to dress up. It was Friday night and I wasn't going to stay home. I grabbed my phone and considered asking Whitney to meet me at The Den but decided against it. I needed to be alone right now.

I had to hold onto the wall of the elevator, but I managed to make it outside without falling. My pleasant buzz had escalated to something more that I wasn't used to experiencing. I had only made it to the end of the block before I heard my name being called. I turned around and saw Lane hurrying toward me. I leaned against the building wall, waiting for him.

"Abby, *what* is going on?" Lane looked so upset. I felt horrible.

I shook my head. A bad idea, since it seemed that my head couldn't keep up with my shaking, causing a throbbing sensation. "Nothing's wrong. You shouldn't be here."

Turning to go, Lane grabbed my arm to stop me. "You don't get the only say on what's going on with us! There are two people in this relationship, and *two* people get to have a say!" His face was angrier than I had ever seen it.

I could feel the tears returning. "But only one of us has a chance at happiness, and I'm trying to give that to you." I ducked my face down, squeezing my eyes so I wouldn't start crying again.

Lane exhaled loudly and pulled me into his arms, hugging me tightly. "Oh, Abby. Let me help you. You make me happy, please don't ever doubt that."

I sank into his embrace, relishing it before pulling away. "But I won't keep you happy if you stay with me." I took a step back, leaving a piece of my heart with him. "You'll come to resent me, I know it." Another step, another piece of my heart.

Lane just stared at me, looking incredulous. "That would never happen."

I held up a hand, cutting him off. "It would. We don't know what's wrong with me. You would come to hate my outbursts and episodes. I can't have you hating me," I whispered, laying down the rest of my heart. It was okay if it was broken. I only wanted to save Lane's from becoming the same.

I turned and walked away, wiping my face off. Lane followed behind, talking to me.

"I'm not giving up on you Abby. On us. We are amazing together and I won't let you make some sort of snap judgment because of whatever happened today."

My tears turned into loud, gasping cries as I picked up my pace, trying to outrun Lane. I should have known I couldn't do that on a good day, let alone when I was drunk and he was sober.

Still determined to reach The Den, I ignored Lane, even though he kept pace with me. I just needed the obliteration of today through the drinking of more beer.

At last, I had had enough. I started walking when the last light turned green and looked to Lane. "Can't you tell when you're not wanted?" I yelled at him.

"Of course, I can! But I know I'm needed here, so I'm trying to help you, damn it!"

I stopped in the middle of the street, turning around to face him. "Look here—"

I didn't have time to finish what I was going to say because the sound of tires squealing muffled it. A red four-door car came racing by where I had just been standing.

Lane grabbed me by the waist and yanked me toward him, out of the path of the car. I screamed and held onto him, fear propelling me into his arms, praying he had been fast enough.

The red car raced off, leaving confusion and fear in its wake. I trembled in Lane's arms, my legs ready to give out.

Lane led me to the opposite sidewalk, where I had been headed before almost being ran over. I sat down roughly, not feeling steady enough to stand anymore. I hung my head in my hands, my head throbbing with my fast heartbeat. "Oh my God, *what* just happened? That was like freaking déjà vu or something."

I felt more than saw Lane stiffen next to me. "Say that again," he said, laying a hand on my arm.

I screwed up my eyebrows in confusion when I looked at him. "Um, what?"

Lane shifted next to me to face me. "Say what you just said again!"

I drew back, my head still feeling muddled from the beer I had drunk. "Okay…I said it feels like déjà vu."

Lane's jaw dropped open. "That's it, Abby. That's what felt so strange about this! Do you realize this is how we met? On this corner, with me pulling you out of the way of a car speeding through a red light!"

I could only stare at him. "You pulled me away both times."

Lane grinned, grabbing my face with both hands. "See! This proves you're not crazy, that there's something going on!"

I shook my head, trying to make sense of it all. "So, what? It's just all coincidence, or is it a message to me? Are you saying it's, like, pre-ordained that I get run over?"

Lane gave me a look. "I'm saying what I've said all along Abigail. I believe you. I believe you and I want to help you. Please, let me."

All I could do was stare at him. This man, who had been so good to me, believed me. Believed that I wasn't crazy, that I wasn't making this up.

"This is so insane," I whispered.

"I know," Lane replied. "But I'm here for you."

More tears came leaking out before I could stop them. "I'm so sorry," I moaned, leaning toward him.

Lane gathered me in his arms, rubbing my back. "Nothing to be sorry for," he said, kissing the top of my head.

Chapter Six

The rest of the night went by without me really feeling a part of it. I was feeling sick to my stomach, thinking about what had happened. A car had almost run me over – *again* – and Lane was there to save me – *again.* And just like he had pointed out, he was there to save me both times.

We stayed at The Den for a while. I needed the time to calm down before heading home.

Downing my second shot, I wiped my mouth off with the back of my hand. My stomach was rolling with a nauseous feeling, not cooperating with what I was wanting. Lane sat across from me, watching me over his glass of beer.

"Want to talk about it?" he offered.

"Nope," I said shortly, taking a drink of my beer. It didn't matter what we had just experienced, I was no good for Lane. He had to see that.

Lane leaned toward me over the high-top, elbows on the table. He reached out a hand to mine, which I retracted. I couldn't let his affection cloud my judgment.

His face hardened as he sat back, forming a fist with his hand. "You can't draw away from me Abby," he said.

I looked down at the table, playing with my napkin, tearing tiny pieces off. "I'm not doing anything."

"What happened today?"

I shrugged, rolling the torn napkin into a ball. "It doesn't matter. It's over."

Lane slapped his hand down on the table, causing the glasses to shake. "Damn it, Abby, *look* at me!"

I threw my head up, startled. The expression on Lane's face scared me. Sadness, anger, and dread were all there, making me feel even worse. I was the cause of this. I was the cause of him feeling so awful.

"I can't," I whispered. "I can't look at you knowing how much I want you here with me but knowing that you have to stay away from me."

Lane's face softened at my confession, his hand reaching back out to capture mine. He stood up, eyes never leaving my face, and walked around to my side of the table.

Moving his hand to gently cup my face, he leaned down toward me, his breath stirring my hair. "I'm *not* leaving, Abby. I love you."

I let out a shaky breath, tears clouding my vision. "You love me?" I asked.

Lane smiled, his thumb caressing my cheek. "I do. I met the girl I never thought I would find. The girl who gets my heart racing, who makes me smile."

He moved closer still, his other arm coming up to trap me in my seat. Kissing my forehead, he whispered, "She somehow burrowed her way into my heart and I'm not about to let her go."

I sighed, resting my head on his chest. "You have such weird taste in women."

Lane barked out a laugh. Hugging me close, he said, "I wouldn't have it any other way."

I nestled into his arms, enjoying the security they provided. Lane rubbed my back before moving away, going to sit down in his seat.

"I'm going to the bathroom. Need anything?" he asked.

I downed the rest of my beer, about half of the glass. "Yep. I need another drink."

Lane narrowed his eyes and looked disapprovingly at my glass but didn't say anything about it. He just nodded and left.

Glancing around the full bar, I let the music and alcohol I had consumed relax me a little more. Closing my eyes, I took a few deep breaths.

Lane had said he *loved* me. Was I supposed to say it back? I wasn't sure yet if I loved him, but I knew I wanted to. I hoped he wasn't upset that I didn't say it back.

Oh, man. He probably was. I sat up, anxiety rolling through me, my heart starting to race again. I was no good at these things, this is why I should leave.

Before I could do anything, a beer was placed in front of me. Turning to thank Lane, I realized it was some big, burly guy who was smirking at me.

"A pretty lady like you shouldn't be left alone on a Friday night," he said, sitting down next to me.

I shifted in my seat uncomfortably. "Oh, uh, thanks, but I'm good. I'm—"

The man cut me off, irritation on his face. "Now, look, I went to the trouble of bringing you a beer. The least you could do is sit here with me and drink it."

I dared a look around but didn't see Lane anywhere. My adrenaline was amped up, but I just found myself frozen to my seat, too scared to move. I slowly reached for the drink, wrapping my fingers around it.

The man grinned. "Now that's more like it." He moved his seat closer to mine, placing an arm on the back of it. "So, what are you doing all on your lonesome tonight?"

"She's not alone."

I heard Lane's voice behind me and turned to face him. The panic I felt must have been plain to see, because Lane moved closer and pushed away the other guy's beer before placing his own plus mine down in front of me. "Is there a problem here?"

The man sat back, looking smug. "No, no problem man. Just having a drink with a pretty lady who was alone."

"Well, she's not alone now," Lane said, his voice hard.

I was only able to sit there, barely able to breathe. *This is not happening*, I thought in disbelief.

These two guys were about to duke it out right in front of me.

Lane looked at me. "Babe, are you wanting to drink with this guy?"

I widened my eyes at him and shook my head no.

Lane slid the man's beer back in front of him. "You heard her. Time to go. Before I get someone over here to make you leave."

The man narrowed his eyes at Lane, but got up, grabbed his drinks and left. I let out an explosive breath that I hadn't realized I was holding. I put a hand up to my chest, hoping that my pounding heart would calm down soon.

Lane sat back down and just looked at me. "I just can't leave you alone, can I, woman?"

My jaw dropped until I saw Lane's lips twitch, trying to fight a smile. I grinned at him and then started laughing. I couldn't help it; all of my anxiety and fear needed an outlet.

Lane just shook his head at me, taking a drink.

"Let's just have a normal night," I suggested. "No talk of my problems. I just want to forget them for the night."

With a nod, Lane picked up his glass. "To forgetting."

I raised my glass too. "To forgetting." With that, I took a big drink.

****

The next morning, I woke up groaning. My mouth felt like it was full of sand and my head was throbbing. I stretched, arching my back, hitting something.

I froze, trying to remember what had happened last night. Drinking with Lane, scary guy, more drinking. Whitney and a friend had ended up joining us. So much drinking. *No wonder I feel so awful*, I thought. I vaguely remembered coming home and undressing to my underwear in front of Lane.

I shifted a little, realizing with relief that I was still dressed. A sigh sounded behind me, an arm wrapping around my waist, pulling me in closer. It took me by surprise until it registered in my alcohol-ridden brain that it was Lane. *And I just bumped my butt into him*, I thought, mortified.

Lying there, I knew I couldn't fall back to sleep. Even if I wanted to get up, Lane's arm was trapping me in, his other arm beneath me. Not that I was complaining. Not at all. His bare chest was warm against my back and his breath was tickling the back of my neck. I snuggled in closer, trying to be careful not to wake him.

This feeling was too perfect. *I could definitely lie here all day*, I thought, knowing it was wishful thinking.

It was then that I noticed Lane's hand was moving, slowly caressing my stomach, sending butterflies fluttering inside me. I didn't move, not wanting him to stop.

"Good morning," he whispered, planting a kiss on my shoulder before placing another one by my neck.

I trembled, pleasure radiating from that sensitive spot. "Good morning yourself," I whispered back.

Lane's hand moved up, leaving a trail of fire across my stomach. His thumb brushed the bottom of my bra, causing me to gasp and arch my back, trying to feel more.

Lane snickered softly, kissing my neck again. His hand moved back down my stomach, fingers lightly grazing my skin.

I tried to turn over to face him, but he held me still with the arm that was below me. "Uh-uh. You don't get to move." Emphasizing his point, he dropped a leg over both of mine.

I tried to control my breathing, so he couldn't hear the gasping that was wanting to escape.

Lane's hand was on my hip, his thumb teasing the edge of my panties, making me grateful I at least had a nice pair on. I wriggled, unable to hold still anymore.

Lane smacked my behind lightly. "Stay still. I'm enjoying myself."

"You could enjoy yourself more if I could *roll over*," I said, squirming more to get a rise out of him.

Lane laughed and flipped me over, kissing me hard. All rational thought left me as his lips took over. I moaned as his tongue gently brushed against mine, wreaking havoc on my attempt to breathe normally.

As we kissed, there was a natural push and pull to our rhythm that came to us. His hand cupped me from behind, hitching my leg over his, fitting our forms together.

I pulled back, looking Lane in the eye. He had the same desperate look on his face that I was sure was on mine. My hand traced his features: across his eyebrow, down his straight nose, over his full lips. My eyes followed my hand, entranced by its actions.

When I finally lifted my eyes back to Lane's, I noticed a desire in them that drew me in. I slowly slid closer, my nose bumping his.

His hand pushed the hair away from my face, ending at the back of my neck, holding me close to him.

"I won't go any further than you're ready for." He brushed his lips gently across mine, sucking in my bottom lip before nipping at it.

I groaned, "You're making it really hard to say no." Leaning back, I kept Lane at a distance. "How did you end up in my bed, anyway?"

He tried to hide his smile. "You don't remember?"

I shook my head. "Only bits and pieces. I guess I took that 'forgetting' toast literally."

Lane smiled at me, shaking his head. "We went through a few drinks and I think you texted Whitney to join us. We stayed until the bar closed, and we came back here. You didn't want me going home drunk and offered for me to stay here. You did a sexy little striptease for me," he said, raising his eyebrows while I died of embarrassment.

He pulled my hands away from my face. "Don't worry, you were amazing. But I'm *not* going to have our first time be while we're drunk and won't remember it."

I let out a soft sigh, laying my head down on his chest. His top hand held me closely, while his other played with my hair, lulling me into a daze.

I wasn't sure how long we lied there, entwined together. Our legs had become puzzle pieces fitted together and our arms were busy caressing each other's bare skin. I breathed in Lane's masculine scent, mixed with his cologne.

Pressing my lips to his chest, I whispered, "I was an idiot last night."

Lane shifted his head back to look at me. "No, you weren't. You were trying to protect yourself, and me. Nothing idiotic about that. You were being selfless. I just want you to let me in, believe that you can trust in me."

I scrunched my face up against the barrage of emotions I was feeling. Relief, that Lane wasn't running, even when I was pushing him away. Anxiety, that I would have to tell him every crazy detail. And there was a last emotion I felt bubbling up that I wasn't sure I was ready to face yet.

"I had another episode yesterday." I rolled onto my back so I wouldn't have to look at Lane. He followed me anyway, leaning up on one elbow to look down at me as I spoke.

Staring at my ceiling, I said, "I went out to lunch with a co-worker to some café. I – I—"

Lane tilted my head to face him and gently kissed me. "Take your time. You're safe here."

Hot tears stung my eyes. I leaned up and kissed him back. "You're too perfect."

Lane chuckled. "I don't know about that. I just know how I feel about you and what I would do for you."

I smiled. "That makes me feel good." I sat up, reveling in the pleasure I felt when Lane's eyes drifted downward to my chest. He gave me a cheeky half-smile when he looked back up.

"I would say I'm sorry, but I'm not," he said, smirking at me.

Pursing my lips, I shook my head. "Typical guy. If your hormones have calmed down, I'm ready to tell you what happened."

Lane put on a serious face. "I'm ready."

I rolled my eyes at his antics, feeling more relaxed than before. "So, like I was saying, I was out to lunch yesterday."

Lane nodded, silently encouraging me to continue.

I took a deep breath. "It was auditory and visual. Hallucinations, I mean. All I could see and hear was 'wake up.' Everywhere. People talking to me, words written down. They were all the same."

Dread filled my stomach, remembering the horrible feelings. I swallowed, trying to repress it.

Lane's look of concern stopped me for a second before I plowed on.

"I think I need a doctor. To do some scans or something. Something is wrong with me."

Lane sat up, wrapping me in his arms, giving me security. "I will be here with you, no matter what."

I laid my head on his shoulder. "You don't know how grateful I am to hear that. But I also don't want you sticking by out of pity."

Lane pushed me back so we could see eye to eye. "Don't be ridiculous. It is *not* pity that I feel for you. I thought I had made that clear. I *love* you. I'm *not* going anywhere."

"You love a crazy girl. Don't deny it," I said when I saw him start to protest.

"Then I won't," he said, smiling. "But you're *my* crazy girl."

"And I wouldn't have it any other way," I said, slowly pushing him back down onto the bed. I hovered over him, searching his face.

Lane smiled at me before drawing me down to him for a kiss. If it was possible, it was even better than before.

Lane's hands drifted down my back, hesitating when he reached the bottom before sliding them down lower, holding me closer to him.

I could feel his arousal under me, taking my mind places as his mouth worked magic on mine. Finally, I pushed away.

"I don't – I'm not – um, I'm not ready," I stammered, feeling a blush creep up my neck to my face.

Lane brushed my hair back, his thumb stroking my cheek. "It's okay. I told you, only as far as you're ready to go. I'm okay with that."

I smiled. "I was right. You are too perfect."

Lane laughed at that. "I believe you're wrong, my dear, but I'll let you keep saying it."

I sat up again, bringing him with me. "I will! Now let's go get some breakfast. I'm starving."

****

The next Wednesday, I was sitting and waiting anxiously at the doctor's office. I had done all of my testing yesterday, and today I would be hearing the results.

I'm going to puke, I thought, wishing my stomach would settle.

Neither Lane nor Whitney had been able to come with me today. I had thought I would be okay until I found myself alone waiting for either good or bad news.

I blinked furiously as tears threatened to fall. I couldn't believe I was alone on such an important day! I took my phone out of my pocket to text Whitney and Lane.

Me: *You suck. You're gonna feel horrible when I come home with bad news*

Whitney was the first to text back.

Whitney: *THINK POSITIVE! You're going to be fine!*

I smiled. I should change my attitude. It couldn't hurt at least. Another text popped up, but before I could read it, the doctor came in, carrying a file.

"Hello, Abigail, I'm Doctor Woods. I've got your test results here if you're ready to go over them."

I swallowed hard, my mouth suddenly dry. Nodding, I said, "Yes, I'm ready."

Dr. Woods nodded and sat back in his desk chair. Opening the file, he flipped through a few pages. "Well, the good news is we didn't find anything."

I slumped over, letting out the breath I was holding. "Oh, thank God," I said. I looked up at him. "Wait, does that mean there's bad news?"

"I'm not sure yet. You were describing some very vivid, detailed things to us yesterday. I'm actually a little surprised that nothing showed up." He leaned forward, closing the file and pushing it to the side. "The hallucinations and dreams you're having mean that something is wrong. Right now, I'd like to prescribe you some anti-anxiety medicine and see if that helps."

I just stared at Dr. Woods, blinking. "Anxiety? You just think it's...anxiety? That I'm so stressed out that I'm causing myself to hallucinate?" I didn't even know how to take that.

"Unfortunately, as of right now, that's the best I have to offer. I'm not going to be offering anything that could potentially harm you with no conclusive evidence of anything physical going on."

I scoffed at that. "Okay, so I'm just to drug myself up and hope for the best?" I rolled my eyes.

Dr. Woods sighed. "I would hope you wouldn't think of it like that. Can you think of anything in your life that might be contributing to your current situation? Anything with your family or friends...boyfriend?"

I wracked my brain, trying to be cooperative, but nothing came to mind. I shook my head. "Nope.

It was literally just out of the blue. I haven't been stressed about anything before this."

"Okay." Dr. Woods grabbed a pad of paper and started writing. "I'm writing your prescription, which should be ready in a couple of hours." He handed it to me and I took it, noticing my hand was shaking.

Dr. Woods smiled gently. "It's going to be okay. I bet once the medicine kicks in and regulates, you'll feel a whole lot better."

I nodded and stood up, gathering my purse. "Thank you, Dr. Woods. I hope this is the answer I've been looking for."

"I'm sure it will help you," he said. "Come back in one month and we'll see how it's going."

"Okay, thank you."

We shook hands and I left, clutching the prescription like a lifeline. *This has to work*, I thought. *It just has to.*

By the time I had gotten through the traffic blocking the roads and made it to the store, it had already been close to one hour. I went to the pharmacy and then wandered around to browse.

Finding myself in the book section like always, I laughed to realize I was in the self-help area.

"This is stupid, these won't help me," I whispered to myself. I grabbed a couple anyway, figuring I could use all the help I could get.

After getting my new medicine and hiding it away, I drove home, hoping to relax. It was afternoon when I arrived, and Whitney wasn't home yet. I grabbed a beer from the fridge, taking a drink on my way to the couch.

Staring at my bag of goodies, I tried to psych myself up. "It's just medicine, it's only going to help me. And if not, I'll just quit. Easy enough. There's nothing wrong with needing some help."

I finally got the courage to take out the bottle and read it. "Well crap, no alcohol. Whoops," I said, looking at my bottle. "Oh well. One won't hurt, right?"

Shrugging, I took another drink. I needed to calm down. I had no idea why I was so nervous. Reaching for my phone, I saw the forgotten text on there. It was from Lane.

Lane: *Abby, I know you'll be okay. There is nothing wrong with you! We can celebrate the good news that I KNOW you're going to get by going to dinner tonight. What do you say?*

Me: *That sounds perfect. Do you want the news now or later?*

Lane: *Now! What happened?*

Me: *Can you talk on the phone?*

It rang almost immediately.

"Hey!" I answered.

"Hey, yourself! So, how did it go?"

"Well, nothing is wrong with me."

"I knew it!" Lane's voice was upbeat.

"Well, hold on there, cowboy. The doctor said they didn't find anything, but he's got me on an anti-anxiety medicine."

Lane exhaled. "Well, that's okay, isn't it? Do you think it will help you?"

I shrugged, even though I knew he couldn't see me. "I'm really not sure. The doctor basically said I was stressing myself out enough to make me hallucinate."

Silence. Then, "Well, that *would* make sense…but how does that explain me?"

"Oh no. Don't tell me I'm making you up too?" I said jokingly.

"Ha, ha. No, I assure you, I'm as real as you are."

"Well good. Although if not, my brain sure does know how to make 'em. But seriously, good point. How *does* this explain you?"

"No idea. It's not like I'm experiencing anything that you are, besides being able to read the note."

"Hmmm. Maybe I can ask Whitney when she gets here."

"Sounds good. So what time should I come get you?"

"Whenever you want! I'm sitting at home right now. *Alone*," I said suggestively.

Lane groaned. "Of course you are, because I'm busy for the next few hours."

I grinned. "Aww, that's too bad. I guess I'll just see you in a few hours then."

"You can count on it."

After saying goodbye, I looked to my medicine again. "Nothing scary about you, is there? I'll just take my dose and be done with it."

I opened the bottle and shook out a pill. I chased it down with my beer. "I'm a horrible patient," I said out loud. "But it's just one beer. It shouldn't hurt anything."

The next thing I knew, Whitney came crashing into the apartment. I winced, covering my ears.

"Why are you being so loud?" I asked, going into the kitchen.

Whitney turned from the table, where she was depositing her work bag and stepped out of her shoes.

"Oh, hey! How was your appointment?"

I felt my face lose color as I realized I never updated Whitney after I had left. "Oh my God, I never texted you! I'm so sorry! It was fine, I'm fine! The doctor said he couldn't find anything on the tests, so he just prescribed an anti-anxiety medicine for me to take."

Whitney hugged me. "That's great news, Abigail! Let's celebrate!" She went to the fridge and got out a beer and her wine. She popped mine open and poured herself a glass.

Handing my drink to me, she clinked it with her glass. "Cheers! To being healthy and not crazy! Just a little anxious!" she laughed.

I laughed with her and took a drink. "Oh shoot, Whitney, I've already taken a pill plus had a beer earlier. I'm not supposed to mix them."

Whitney waved her hand, dismissing me. "One night won't hurt. It's barely in your system anyhow. You'll be fine!"

I just looked at her, unsure. She tipped my drink up to my lips, forcing me to either drink it or let it spill.

"See, that wasn't so bad!"

"Fine, Whitney, one drink! By the way, I'm meeting up with Lane tonight. He's coming by in a few hours."

Whitney leaned against the kitchen counter, looking at me. "Is he coming to *celebrate* with you?" She leered at me.

"Oh wow, Whitney, no!" I busted out laughing. "There has been no *celebrating* going on."

Whitney pouted. "For real? He's a delectable morsel, don't let him waste away."

I choked on my drink, coughing as it burned in my nose. Whitney rushed over to pat me on the back while I grabbed a towel to wipe my face off with.

"You're ridiculous and impossible. If any...celebrating...were to happen, you know I would tell you," I said, my face blushing to a new shade of red.

Whitney laughed. "I'm just teasing! I'm just wishing I was having more luck with Luke at work."

I smiled at her. "Don't worry. No guy can resist your charm."

She smirked. "True. I'll be patient. Now, what are you planning on wearing tonight?"

I looked down at my jeans and t-shirt. "I'm guessing you're not going to let me wear this?"

Whitney shook her head. "Oh, no. You're going to go shave your legs, put on heels, and knock Lane off his feet."

Rolling my eyes, I turned to march down the hall. "Yes, mom," I called back sarcastically.

Later, Whitney was behind me curling my hair. "There," she proclaimed. "That's the last bit. Stand up, let's see it."

I stood up, showing off the burgundy dress Whitney had found in her closet. The spaghetti straps showed off my arms and more of my chest than I usually did while the mid-thigh length showcased my long legs, and my feet were clad in black heels.

I glanced at Whitney to see her reaction. She was looking me up and down, scrutinizing my appearance. She came to stand in front of me. "You look stunning."

I could've sworn I saw a proud tear in her eye. "Thanks, Whitney."

The sound of knocking on the front door interrupted us. A thrill of excitement danced through me.

I opened the door and Lane took a step back, examining me. I nervously waited for him to look back up. When he did, the look in his eyes told me everything I needed to know. Stepping closer to him,

I gave him a slow kiss, drinking in the rousing scent that he always had.

"Ahem!" Whitney coughed behind us. "If you two are quite finished, Abigail, here's your purse."

I took it from her, whispering, "Thank you," and left with Lane. He drove us to a steakhouse in the heart of the city that I had never been to before.

Over drinks and dinner, we discussed my tests and what the doctor said. I kept worrying about the medicine I had taken but tried to relax and remember what Whitney had said about it barely being in my system.

But by the end of dinner, I was feeling more inebriated than I should have for the two glasses of wine that I had drunk.

"Lane, I'm not feeling too hot," I said, hearing my speech slur. I looked over at him, but the room was starting to spin. "Not good at all."

Lane's brows furrowed, and he reached over to grab my hand, steadying me. "All right. Let's get you home."

I nodded weakly and stood up with Lane's help. Nausea was building in my stomach, but I swallowed it back down, refusing to look weak again in front of him.

At the apartment, Lane waited in the living room while I got my tank top and pajama shorts on. I went back out to him and slumped next to him on the couch.

"I'm a horrible date," I whined into his shoulder.

Lane chuckled, rubbing my arm. "You were great. I wouldn't have figured two glasses of wine would do you in though."

I shook my head against him. "Stupid Whitney. She said it was okay to drink even though I took my medicine earlier."

Lane pushed me away from him. "You mixed them? Should we go to the hospital?"

I clumsily patted his cheek. "You're so cute. I think I just need sleep." I tried to lay down against him again.

"Okay, Sleeping Beauty, I think you'll like your own bed better than me." He got us up and walked us to my room.

"Hmmm, nope. I want to sleep with *you*." I giggled as he laid me down and covered me up.

"How about I stay with you until Whitney is home?"

I tried to answer him, but the darkness was already pulling me under.

I looked around in my dream. I was in the middle of the street, cars racing by me. Surprisingly, I wasn't scared. It's like I knew what would happen. I saw one car coming my way and started to step in front of it when I heard screaming behind me.

I turned around and saw Lane running toward me, yelling at me to stop. I smiled and lifted my hand in a wave right before the car reached me.

The next time I looked around, I was lying down. My mom was leaning over me. "Oh good, you're awake."

"I am?" I asked. Everything had a fuzzy edge to it.

"Why are you asking me?" She turned to me, her face morphing into a terrifying mask of anger. "If you can't tell, then I'll help you!"

She grabbed me with fingers stretched out like talons and started shaking me roughly. "Wake up, Abigail! Wake up, Abigail!" Laughter followed that outburst while my head snapped back and forth.

I sat up, screaming, arms flailing to beat her back.

"Abby, stop! It's just a nightmare!" Lane's arms wrapped around me as my gasps turned into loud cries.

"Oh God, it felt so real Lane," I cried, choking on my tears. I held on tightly to him, using him to anchor me.

Slowly, the tears abated, and my breathing calmed down. Lane's hands were rubbing my back, soothing me further. He laid me down and brought the covers back up. Wiping my face off, he said, "No need to be afraid. I'm here with you."

I smiled and held his hand as I drifted off to sleep again, with no dreams to trouble me for the rest of the night.

Chapter Seven

I woke up feeling refreshed, the horrible dream already receding to the back of my mind. Lane was no longer here, but I saw a note on my side table in his handwriting.

Abigail,

I hope your bad dreams stayed away. I left after I heard Whitney come in and when I was sure you had settled down for the night. I'll talk to you tomorrow. I love you.

Lane

I got up to dress and get breakfast started. While drinking a cup of coffee, I contemplated my previous night and the crazy dream I'd had.

Damn you, Whitney, I thought, shaking my head. I was never going to listen to her advice again. I was getting off the crazy train and not drinking while taking my meds again.

In my dream I had let myself be run over. At least, that's how it had seemed. *But why would I do that?* I thought. I knew I didn't have any control over my dreams, but I also knew I wasn't suicidal.

And then the part with my mom. I shuddered. I can't believe my brain had turned her into some sort of monster. It had scared me half to death.

Sitting at the table with my plate, I thought about it all. Obviously, I had been messed up enough to go crazy in the dream world. Maybe I was too stressed out, like the doctor had said. I wished I could take more time off work, but I had just missed two days to do my testing and meet the doctor.

I decided to look over all of the evidence Lane, Whitney, and I had gathered a few weeks ago.

After cleaning my plate, I took my papers from their drawer and sat back to look them over. First, I read the note again:

If you're reading this, you've been in a coma for almost five years now. We're trying a new technique. We don't know where this message will end up in your dream, but we hope we're getting through. Please wake up! We miss you.

Okay, still weird. Five years ago would make me twenty years old. My mind still rebelled against the thought of me being in a coma. I could feel things, I ate, I breathed, I even dreamed! How do you dream within a dream?

I rubbed my head; the foolishness of the situation was getting out of hand. I smoothed my hair back, going to the notes we made.

Lane could see the note. Nobody else could. Which, as Lane had pointed out, did not support Dr. Woods' suggestion of me stressing myself out.

My migraines started five years ago. Which went along with the coma theory.

The hallucinations. Okay, those could go either way. I was stressed and hearing things, or this was more attempts to get me out of the coma.

I can't get hold of my mom. I wasn't sure where to place that one.

Looking at my stress versus coma list I had made, the coma side was winning.

"What the hell is happening to me?" I whispered, hanging my head in my hands. Could this really be happening? Was the note true?

My head was really starting to hurt. It's like I was trying to figure out how quantum physics and blackholes worked. That's what I felt like while trying to come to terms with this being the truth.

Whitney came into the kitchen. "What are you doing?" She leaned over my shoulder, reading my newly made list. She picked it up. "Abigail, what is this?"

I shrugged, sighing. "I'm trying to come to terms that this note could be true."

Whitney sat down next to me, putting the papers back down. "Hey, don't go there. Do you think *I'm* made up too? Or Lane?"

I looked up at her and saw the hurt on her face. "Of course not!" I cried out, grabbing her hand to hold. "But what else am I supposed to think? I'm sinking here, Whitney! I'm sinking, and I can't find the surface and I don't know if I can pull myself out!"

Whitney sat there, a stunned look on her face. "God, Abigail, I'm sorry. I just want to help you, and I don't know how. I'm not – I mean, I can't be just a figment of your imagination, you know? I have dreams, hopes, things I want, guys I like! Is your brain really that elaborate?"

I giggled, sniffing back my tears. "I don't know what the right answer here is Whitney."

"And think of Lane. Okay, I could probably give you that one. If I could make up a guy like that, then I would in a heartbeat," she said, laughing.

I joined in, laughing and wiping away my tears. "Okay, so what you're saying is that you're real and I've made up Lane?"

Whitney snorted. "Sure, we can go with that."

I looked at my list. "Am I crazy to even consider this? When we first talked about it, I was convinced there was no way it was possible. But now..." I trailed off. "But now, with everything that's been happening..."

I huffed out a breath. "It's spiraling out of control. I'm constantly hit with new things. I just want it to stop."

Whitney knelt in front of me and pulled me to her for a hug. I leaned into it, needing the comfort.

"It'll be okay, Abigail. I am here for you no matter what you need." She shifted back so she could wipe my eyes. "Now, go get ready for work. You can't be getting fired from your pretend job."

I laughed again, grateful that Whitney could show me the humor in the situation.

Later at work, I sat at my desk reading. It was taking everything in me to concentrate. My mind kept wandering.

I was back at square one. Why was this happening to me? I didn't deserve this. I was having an amazing life before this happened. I loved my job, I loved my best friend, and I loved—

I sat up suddenly, dropping my pen. I loved Lane. Oh, wow. I flushed at the sudden rush of emotions flooding through me. I dropped my head into my hands.

I'm such an idiot, I thought. *Why did I have to wait so long to realize this! He's been telling me he loves me for days and I don't even give him a hint that I might feel the same!*

I looked up at the ceiling, hoping for some sort of sign that I wasn't as dumb as I felt. Was there even a length of time where it got to be too long to reciprocate such feelings?

I looked around the office to make sure nobody else was noticing the miniature breakdown I was having. Fortunately, everybody was absorbed in their work. Like I should have been.

Glancing back at my desk, I tried to concentrate on my manuscript. I had a new one, which I was grateful for. I didn't think I could have handled finding any new notes that were mysteriously left for me.

After a few minutes, I realized that I was reading the same paragraph repeatedly. My cheeks were starting to ache with the pull of the grin that kept popping up. I loved Lane. I was in love!

What an incredible feeling. It was like I could float away, and my problems were tiny insignificant things that didn't need my attention. I kept imagining Lane's face as I told him, changing the scenario often.

I would tell him tonight. At dinner. No, wait, it should be a private thing. At the apartment. No, what if Whitney was there? She would make a huge deal about it and embarrass me.

Laying my head down on my desk, I sighed. Why was this so hard for me? I mean, Lane just popped out and said it! At a bar, of all places! I should be able to do the same. Just be casual about it.

Except this wasn't casual. It was the deepest of feelings I could possibly have for a man. I was giving him my heart, and with that, the potential to break it.

I'm overthinking this, I thought. I got my phone out.

Me: *Whitney, I need guy help! Please don't make fun of me!*

Whitney: *Never! What's up?*

Me: *I may or may not have just realized I'm in love with Lane*

Whitney: *OMG! Really? That's so awesome! What's the problem?*

I tried to think of how to phrase my question, then decided to just be blunt.

Me: *How do I tell him? I've never done this before!*

I could just imagine Whitney rolling her eyes at me.

Whitney: *Abigail, sweetie, just tell him! I bet he can't wait to hear it! Maybe you'll get lucky!*

My cheeks flushed, and I looked around quickly, even though I knew nobody could see our texts.

Me: *Okay, thanks, BYE!*

Whitney sent back a winking smiley face, making me smile in response. As much as it scared me, she was right. Just do it.

"After work," I said to myself. "I'll do it tonight."

"Do what tonight?"

I looked up to see Julie hovering over my desk, apparently eager for new gossip. She really needed to get a boyfriend who could keep her distracted from everyone else's business.

Struggling to keep my eyes from rolling, I turned in my chair to face her. "Oh, nothing huge. Just, um, planning dinner for my roommate and me."

Julie's face fell when she heard nothing juicy. "Oh, that's…fun," she said. "So, are you taking your lunch break soon?"

I didn't want to face another possible breakdown with her again, so I shook my head. "No, I'm not. I've got catching up to do since I missed a couple days," I said, gesturing at my desk.

Julie nodded. "Okay. I'll just see you later then." She waved and walked off, grabbing her purse on the way out.

I felt bad about lying, but man, Julie didn't know when to stop when it came to guys. It was just easier to fib than get strapped down to that type of conversation. *Plus*, I thought as I looked glumly at my work, *I really do have a lot of catching up to do.*

The rest of the day I spent chained to my desk. I didn't even leave for lunch, instead grabbing a few snacks and a Diet Coke from the vending machines to munch on. I had gotten into a groove, that zone where I got so focused that nothing could have distracted me.

The next time I looked up, it was nearly five o'clock and time to leave. I packed up my bag, tidying up the papers that I had taken notes on and scattered around my desk.

"I'm so glad tomorrow is a short day," I said to myself, once again grateful for the company policy of leaving early on Fridays.

I drove home and saw Whitney on the living room couch. She jumped up and intercepted me before I could go into the room.

"Abigail! You're here!"

I looked at her as if she had grown an extra head. "Of course, I'm here, Whitney. I do live here after all."

I tried to walk around her, but Whitney side-stepped in front of me again, stopping me.

"Oh, I know, I just meant, um, you're here *now*," she stammered.

"Well," I said, trying to walk again, "it *is* after five. Work is done, so I had nothing better to do than come home. Okay, Whitney, *what* are you doing?" She kept blocking my every step.

Whitney stepped forward, grabbing my hands. "Okay, don't panic, but Lane's here."

"Why would I—"

She interrupted me. "No, I know, but he found your notes. Your *theory* notes. I get the feeling he's not too happy with the direction you're leaning."

Understanding dawned on me. "Oh. *Oh.* Is it that bad?" I whispered, wringing my hands together.

"It's hard to tell. He's got a look on his face though," she said.

I straightened my shoulders. "Okay, this should *not* be that big of a deal. I'm going to go see what he says."

I took a few tentative steps, then turned to look at Whitney. All she had to offer me was a thumbs-up and encouraging smile.

I scowled at her before turning and marching into the living room. Lane was sitting in the recliner. That was already a bad sign. He always sat on the couch, so he could be near me and hold me.

"Hey, Lane," I said, going to sit down on the couch.

"Hey, Abigail," he said.

Full name. Was he really that upset?

"What's up? I wasn't expecting you over tonight."

Lane ran a hand through his hair, a gesture I had fast learned meant he wasn't happy.

"I was going to surprise you tonight. Come hang out with you here. I, uh, found your papers on the kitchen table."

Crap. I had totally forgotten about them after my talk with Whitney this morning.

"Okay," I said slowly. "Is there something wrong?"

Lane blew out a breath. "I don't know. Maybe? I'm trying to be understanding and supportive. But, Abby, how could you even think like this?"

I opened and closed my mouth a few times, unable to form an answer. How did I explain my feelings to someone who had no clue what I was going through? Even though Whitney was supportive of me, I also knew she was only trying to placate me in hopes I would get a grip on myself.

I shrugged, still trying to come up with the right words. "I don't know. I don't, okay! But what else am I supposed to think anymore? I'm not crazy, Lane. I can't be. Besides, these episodes are all pointing to the same thing."

"What, they're all giving you the same message that you're in a coma? That you've made all this up?" He spread his hands wide as if to encompass the whole world.

"So, you're telling me this is all in your head. That you couldn't just go out right now, buy an airplane ticket and travel across the world? Does your coma world even exist that far? Or does everything turn blank at the city limit sign?"

I blinked back tears. I had never seen Lane like this. He had never spoken harshly to me, even when I was trying to break up with him.

"How should I know?" I cried, wiping my face of the rebellious tears that I couldn't contain. "What does it even matter, it doesn't even affect you!"

Lane stood up suddenly. "What? Doesn't affect me, are you serious? This most certainly does affect me, Abigail! I'm your boyfriend! I am *not* a figment of your imagination!"

I stood up, too. "That's not what I mean Lane! I meant that I'm the one living with it! I'm the one who's seeing things and hearing things and passing out and who knows what it'll be next time!"

Lane sneered at me. "Oh, you're the one living with it? Well, let me tell you, I'm living with it, too. I'm dealing with you breaking down all the time or crying everywhere. I'm living with it, too!" he yelled at me.

I took a couple steps back. I couldn't believe this was the same sweet guy who had swept me off my feet. Tears were streaming down my face.

I took a deep breath to steady myself. "You *deal* with me? Is that all I am to you now, a damn charity case?" My breaths were coming short and fast now. I knew I needed to calm down before I started hyperventilating. Nothing was coming out right.

"Of course, you're not a charity case to me, Abigail, but look around you! This is the real world! *I* am real!" He stepped in front of me, grabbing my hands to place on his face, framing it. "*I* am real."

I stepped away from him, too hurt by his comments to take in the wounded expression on his face. I didn't care if I hurt him, he had done his part in this.

"I will not be pitied by anyone," I said. "Especially not by you!"

"Abby, listen to me."

"No!" I screamed. "You don't get to talk to me like that and expect to get away with it! I deserve better!"

I felt hands on my shoulders and turned to see Whitney, her eyes narrowed.

"Lane, I think you should go. Now," she said.

He looked back and forth between the two of us, but I looked away, unable to meet his eyes. My heart was breaking, but I didn't want him to see that.

"Abby, please."

Whitney didn't let him get any further. "I said leave, Lane!"

He nodded slowly, grabbing his jacket from the arm of the recliner. He walked to the door and stood there for a second before turning to me. "I love you, Abby. Please don't forget that. I'm so sorry." He opened the door and stepped through it. The click of the latch was like a hit to my heart.

Whitney and I stood there for a second while I tried to process everything.

"I was going to tell him I loved him today," I whispered, stunned. I couldn't stop staring at the door where my heart had just left.

"I gave my heart and soul to him, even if he didn't know it. I never got the chance to tell him, Whitney." My voice cracked as the pain came rushing to me all at once.

The tears came faster than I expected. I bent over, unable to stand up straight as I cried, the weight of my sorrow too much to bear. Whitney rubbed my back, murmuring soothing words to me.

Unbidden memories came flashing to me as I stood there and wept. The first time I met Lane all the way up until he told me he loved me.

With that memory in my head, I crumpled to the ground, all my strength gone. I folded my arms around my head, trying to protect myself from Whitney's gaze.

I wasn't sure how long I lied on the floor of our living room, crying out all the anguish that was tearing through me. How had it come to this? Why couldn't Lane see what he was doing? Why didn't he come back for me?

I wasn't even sure I wanted him to come back. The things he had said, the anger on his face, all those things tore me to my core.

Eventually, I came out of my stupor to realize Whitney was still sitting beside me, rubbing my back. My head was pounding with the force of my breakdown. My nose was stuffed up, but running profusely, and my head was getting worse by the minute.

"Whitney," I said sluggishly, my face still pressed into the floor.

"I'm here, Abigail. What do you need?" she answered, leaning down over me.

The pounding in my skull was starting to make its way to the left side of my head, causing me to groan loudly.

"Whitney, it's happening. My head. Another migraine," I slurred. My eyes were going blurry.

"Shit, um, okay. Can you stand, and I'll help you to your bed?" she asked.

I tried moving and slowly got to my hands and knees, hanging my head down against the nausea building in my stomach.

Whitney helped me stand, wrapping her arms around me for support, letting me lean on her. We walked to my room, where I practically fell onto my bed, moaning as another shot of pain lanced through my skull.

"Can I get you anything?" Whitney asked, sounding nervous. It had been a while since she'd had to deal with me and my migraines.

Tears leaked from my eyes as I squeezed them shut, silently praying to pass out soon so I wouldn't have to feel anything.

"Just stay with me a while?" I whispered, finally feeling darkness steal over me.

I never heard Whitney's response as I slipped away into nothingness. The first thing I noticed when I opened my eyes was that I was outside.

What in the hell? I wondered, looking around.

I had seen this place before, weeks ago. I was back in that abandoned city. No cars, no people, just…nothing.

I turned in a circle, hoping for *something*, but not sure what. That damned payphone was back on its corner, taunting me.

Why was I back here? I had never dreamed during my migraines before. Why now?

The payphone started ringing, making me jump. "Screw you!" I yelled at it. I wasn't playing this game again.

I started walking up the street, hoping for some clue on how to wake up. Maybe I just had to wait it out. Turning the corner, I froze. Another payphone was on this block, too.

I turned around and crossed the street, walking away from it. But it didn't matter what I did or how far I walked. That payphone was on every corner I turned on to.

"What do you want from me?" I yelled at the sky. I threw my arms out, turning in a circle. I knew how ridiculous I looked, but I couldn't help myself.

I walked up to the building I was in front of and tried the door. To my surprise, it opened with ease. Going inside, I looked around. It appeared to be a hotel lobby, a reception desk to my right and an open waiting area on the left, decorated with plush chairs and couches. I could see a dining area to the back, every place fully set with fancy chinaware.

Slowly entering the lobby, I kept glancing around me, not sure of what I was expecting to happen here. I huffed. I shouldn't be so scared! This was my dream, wasn't it? I should be able to control what happened here.

Except, deep down, I knew this wasn't a normal dream. And that scared me.

I walked down the hallway leading to the elevators. Eyeing them warily, I hesitated. Could they get stuck with me on them? I didn't want to take the risk.

The stairwell was right beside the elevators, and I opened the door. It was pitch black except for the red exit signs glowing at each door.

Creepy, I thought. *Never mind.*

I turned to head back outside but was blocked by a wall that hadn't been there a minute ago. Looking around, I noticed the hallway had turned into a tiny room, with no doors. The elevators and stairwell were my only exit.

Chills crept up my spine at this twist. This felt menacing. Like something was playing with me.

Shuddering, I walked to the stairwell door. That was definitely a no-brainer. I wasn't about to get on that elevator and get stuck. Or worse, be taken somewhere against my will that I couldn't stop.

Opening the door, I stepped in, letting my eyes adjust to the gloominess. With nothing to prop the door open, I reluctantly let it fall shut. The slam echoed around me, travelling upward.

I put one foot on the first step, looking up to the next floor landing.

"This sucks," I said, climbing to what I was sure was my doom.

The second-floor door was locked. Looking up, I tried to make out how many more glowing exit signs I could see, but lost track at three. The lights seemed to fade the higher up they were.

I was halfway up the next flight when I heard a scuffing noise below me. I leaned over the railing, trying to place where it was coming from. I heard it again, accompanied by a hissing. It sounded like it was heading my way.

"Oh, hell no," I said, running up the stairs now.

The hissing was growing louder, and I cried out, imagining whatever thing that noise came from was right behind me. I yanked open the next door, falling to the ground as the door clanged shut behind me.

I gasped for air, huddling on the floor, but the door stayed shut. I risked a glance around. I was in a brightly lit hallway, an endless row of doors to my left and right.

I slowly stood up, using the wall to support me.

"Now what's going on?" I wondered. When was this nightmare going to end?

I briefly toyed with the idea of playing "eenie-meenie-miney-moe" on which direction to take, but just chose to go to my right instead. I trailed my hand along the wall as I walked, reluctant to try any of the doors.

I heard a phone ringing a few doors down on my left. It completely unnerved me to think that the payphone had followed me up here.

Shadows suddenly crossed in front of me, and I turned around, dread pooling in my stomach.

The lights were shutting off behind me, one by one.

In the back of my head, I knew where I had to go, but I balked at the idea. But I also didn't want to be in this hallway when those lights went out. Instinctively, I knew I wouldn't be safe out here once there were no lights left.

A hissing sounded behind me from the shadows, and I gasped. My hands became clammy as fear drove me to the door with the ringing phone.

I eased it open, glancing inside. Looking over my shoulder to make sure nothing was following me, I stepped in, locking the door just to be safe.

The room was plain. Just a bed on the right-hand side with a table next to it. I ignored the phone sitting on it. A window was on the wall across from me and I walked to it. I was about five stories up and the same barren landscape I had walked in before faced me again now.

The ringing eventually drew my attention away from the window. Going to stand in front of the phone, I sat down on the bed.

I knew I was just delaying the inevitable. This whole dream world had obviously been designed to lead me to this place.

I picked up the phone, unsure that I wanted to hear what was on the other line.

"H – hello?"

"There's been no change," a voice said.

"Hello? Who is this?"

"I suggest extreme actions," the voice said.

I sat there, trying to decipher the conversation.

"You need to kill that one."

Kill who? I pulled the phone away from my ear and stared at it as if it could tell me what kind of conversation I was listening in on.

Who was talking? Who needed to be killed? Was somebody about to be murdered? Somebody I knew? I didn't want to hear anymore.

I slammed the phone down, scared to listen to more. I laid down on the bed, allowing my emotions to wash over me.

All the tears I had been holding in came gushing out, shocking me by their force. I had held in so much. I sobbed, my chest heaving as I let out all my anger, sadness, and fear. My eyes were starting to feel raw and swollen from me rubbing them, and the pillow was becoming stained with my tears and the drainage from my nose that I couldn't sniff back.

I drifted into an uneasy sleep, the tears slowing but never ceasing. Small tremors shook me as my breathing started to regulate again.

A hand stroked my hair, comforting me. "Shh, Abigail. You're okay now. Shh."

I opened my eyes and blinked a few times, clearing the tears from them. I looked around and saw that I was back in my own room, and Whitney was sitting on the bed beside me.

"Am I awake?" I croaked. I winced, clearing my throat.

Whitney smiled. "Yeah, you are. You've been out for a few hours, but I came in when I heard you crying in your sleep. Bad dream?"

I thought back to the crazy experience I had just gone through, ending with the phone voice saying somebody was going to die. Was it a premonition? Or just something my migraine-driven brain had conjured up to torment me?

I nodded, unable to form the words I needed. "Yeah. Bad dream."

"Well, how about if you're feeling better, I go and cook you some soup? And I'll go and get you some headache medicine while I'm out there."

I nodded again, although I was pretty sure that I didn't need it. My migraine had passed, and my head felt perfectly fine again. No more blinding fire rushing through it, making me feel completely helpless. I was fine. Just fine.

Wasn't I?

Whitney got up, patting me on the arm before leaving my room. I slowly rolled over, my stomach still heaving a little as I moved. I grabbed my phone from my nightstand and opened it. There were four missed calls and a few texts, all from Lane.

Drawing on the courage I wasn't totally sure I had, I opened his text messages.

Lane: *I'm so sorry. Please forgive me*

Lane: *I just need to know if you're okay*

Lane: *I've tried calling, but no answer. Or maybe that is your answer?*

The last one was from about thirty minutes ago.

Lane: *I just called Whitney. She said you were down with a migraine. I can't help but feel like that's my fault.*

I snorted.

You were so upset when I left. I said horrible things to you. Things that should have never crossed my thoughts. I'm just scared. Scared for you and scared of the depths of my feelings for you. I've never felt so much for someone before. You take my breath away with everything you do and say. I love you. I can't begin to tell you how so very sorry I am. Please, please forgive me. I don't want to lose you.

I wiped away a few tears that had fallen as I read Lane's apology. I wasn't sure I was ready to forgive him though. I decided to wait until tomorrow to write him back. I needed a clear head, and I knew I would write with my emotions if I texted him now.

Soon enough, Whitney came back with soup for me to eat. I managed to eat about half of it and gave the bowl back to her.

"There now, just rest. You should be okay by morning."

I laid back down and let Whitney cover me up. But I knew I wasn't going to be fine.

Because somebody was going to die.

Chapter Eight

Breakfast the next morning was a melancholy affair. I stared dejectedly into my bowl of cereal, scooping it up and letting it plop back off my spoon.

"Okay, enough, this is too depressing." I heard Whitney say. "Have you not talked to Lane yet?"

I shook my head, both to answer her and to keep my tears at bay. I had shown her his messages earlier, hoping for some insight on what I should do next. She hadn't been much help.

"Maybe you should just answer him. He seems really sorry."

I glared at her. "You're supposed to be on my side, remember? Besides, he said some horrible things. He just *deals* with me and my issues."

I pushed away my cereal, too upset to try to keep pretending to eat. Standing up, I took it to the sink and poured it out.

"Are you ever going to put him out of his misery?"

I hung my head, tears pricking my eyes while I took in a shallow breath. Sniffing lightly, I said, "I will. I don't know when or how. But I will."

Whitney just watched me, waiting to see what I would do next.

"I'm fine, Whit. Trust me. I just want to go to work and forget any of this ever happened." I wiped my hands off on a towel and turned to her. "How am I supposed to get over this though? How do I just forget he said those things?" Heat rushed through my eyes and nose as more tears appeared.

Whitney stood up and came over, embracing me. "It's hard. Once things are said, they can't be taken back. Good or bad. And what he said, those weren't good things. But I think they were also said emotionally and in the heat of the moment. He loves you Abigail. Take the time to hear him out and make him apologize in person. You deserve that much, and so does he."

I nodded. "You're right. Maybe I can see if he wants to meet for lunch or something."

Whitney patted me on the shoulder. "Great idea. Now go clean up and get ready for work. Wear something hot so he can feel even worse."

I laughed, happy to be feeling a little better. "You're brilliant. I'm going to go find something to wear."

Which was apparently easier said than done. I had been standing inside of my closet for almost ten minutes trying to find the perfect outfit to wear. I sighed, wishing I could go shopping before work. Finally, I grabbed my black pencil skirt and a turquoise, silky button-up shirt. My black heels would complete the outfit.

After putting on some makeup, I grabbed my work bag and headed back out to the living room. Whitney looked up from the couch and whistled at me. "You look hot! And that skirt," she said, giving me the A-Okay sign with her fingers. "You'll definitely knock him dead."

I turned around and stuck my butt out at her. "So, you're saying I should accidentally drop something and pick it up in front of him?" I laughed.

Whitney laughed and shook her head. "Hey, whatever it takes to make him feel even worse!"

I waved goodbye and left, driving to work. Heading to my desk, I unloaded my bag, setting everything up just as I liked it. Satisfied, I turned to my phone, re-reading Lane's messages.

Me: *I got your messages. Do you want to meet for lunch?*

Now just to wait. My stomach was in knots waiting for his reply. It was really starting to make me feel sick. Maybe I should have eaten more for breakfast. Or more than just cereal. I definitely needed a heartier meal before I tried to face Lane.

Laying my head in my hands, I took a deep breath. "It's going to be okay, it's going to be okay," I chanted, trying to convince myself that it was true. Why was this so hard for me? Probably because I had never been in love with someone before, and I didn't care so much about fights with previous boyfriends.

My phone chimed, startling me out of my misery.

Lane: *I would love to do lunch. When can we meet?*

I looked at my clock, debating on how long it would take me to finish my work before I could leave to eat.

Me: *How about we meet around one? I don't think I can get out of here before then*

Lane: *That's perfect. I hope you're doing okay*

I stared at his message, unsure of how to respond. Yes, I was fine, so I wasn't affected by his outburst last night. No, I wasn't fine, so I was breaking down and crying over him. This was not a win-win situation for me.

Me: *I'm as okay as I can be*

That would have to do for now. I couldn't trust myself to keep texting and not spill my guts to him. That would have to wait until I could see him in person at lunch.

I didn't hear any more from Lane, thankfully. It helped me concentrate on my work. Whitney sent me a few texts asking if I was okay, plus another picture of her co-worker, Luke. This time it was a selfie of them together and not a sneaky one.

I smiled at it and texted her a thumbs-up back. It seemed like she was making progress with him if he was in her pictures now and not just in the background.

At 12:45, I was able to slow things down and come to a stopping point so I could leave. Instead, I just sat there, working up the nerve to go meet Lane. My mouth was dry, and my palms were sweating just thinking about it. Wiping my hands off, I shakily stood up. *I can do this. I can do this*, I thought to myself, hoping to give myself the courage to keep my head up tall.

The elevator seemed to speed down to the first floor faster than normal, but I knew that was probably just my imagination. As I stepped out, I realized too late that Lane and I had never agreed on a place to meet. *How stupid of me.* I got my phone out and started writing him a text asking him where to meet.

"Abby?"

I looked up, a stab of fear coursing through me before I recognized Lane standing before me. "Lane? What are you doing here?"

I saw hurt flash through his eyes before his brow straightened back out. "I thought we were going to lunch. Is that not happening anymore?"

I nodded. "Yes, it is. I just thought I was meeting you there. Wherever there was, I guess. I was about to text you to see where you wanted to eat."

Lane smiled. "Well, luckily for you, I'm here to escort you to our destination." He held out his arm for me to take.

I looked at it and then at him, unsure of myself around him now. And I hated that. I used to be so comfortable with him. With our fight last night, I felt like our bond was broken.

Lane's smile faltered, and he started to lower his arm. I stepped up quickly and placed my hand in his arm.

"Thank you. I appreciate it."

He placed his other hand on mine and squeezed it. "Come on. We can go to the café that's a block down from here."

We walked in silence, my heels clicking on the pavement. I couldn't think of any ice breakers to start a conversation, so I just kept my mouth shut, inwardly cringing at how much worse this could go.

By the time we reached the restaurant, I was sweating bullets. The stress of our eventual conversation was getting the best of me. Lane pulled out a chair for me and then sat himself.

He looked at me over the table while I pretended to read the menu. But, of course he could see right through me.

"How are you, really?" he asked.

I shrugged, not able to look him in the eye. "I'm okay. I had another migraine last night, but other than that, I'm fine."

He reached for my hand, grasping it tightly. "Abby, please. I'm so sorry. Really, I didn't mean what I said last night. I don't just deal with you and I hope you know that. I said those things out of frustration."

I looked at his face, full of sincerity. "I can understand that. I do. But it's like that saying: behind every joke is a kernel of truth. You may say you didn't mean those things, but there has to be something in you that believes it."

Lane frowned at me. "I don't, Abby. I'm sorry I hurt you. And that I probably caused your migraine too. All I did was hurt you last night and I never want to do that again. I love you."

My heart swelled again at hearing his admission of love. The apology helped too. I could feel my defenses crumbling down. "I love you, too," I whispered.

Lane sat up straight and grinned at me. "You do?"

I nodded. "Yeah, I do. I was going to tell you last night, but then...well, it didn't go so well for us."

Lane got up and pulled his chair around to my side of the table. Pulling me in toward him for a hug, he stroked my hair and whispered in my ear, "Please forgive me. I'm an ass."

I choked out a laugh and nodded. "You are."

Lane leaned back and looked at me with a twinkle of amusement in his eyes. "I am what? Forgiven or an ass?"

I tilted my head, giving him my best teasing look. "That's probably still up for debate," I said, smirking at him. "But for argument's sake, we'll just say you're forgiven."

Lane leaned in and kissed me, bringing a spark of heat to my belly, spreading outward. Before I could respond, he was gone and back around to his side of the table.

The rest of lunch went more smoothly than I had planned on. Now that things were back to normal between us, I found myself having a fun time.

"So, how's the job search going?" I asked him. "Still searching, right?"

Lane smiled. "Yeah, still searching. Nothing is really popping out at me right now though. And my brother isn't having any luck either."

I wrinkled my nose. "But then how do you pay for things?" My eyes widened. "Oh gosh, that was rude wasn't it? I'm sorry, you don't have to answer that. I have a big mouth."

Lane gave a short laugh. "It's fine. We had some money saved up because we knew we weren't going to have jobs right away and it might take some time to find something. So, we were prepared."

"Oh okay, makes sense. Well, hopefully you find something soon."

"Thanks, Abby. How's your job going?"

"It's going okay now. Now that I'm not getting weird life-changing notes in the middle of my manuscripts," I said sarcastically.

Lane pressed his lips together as if he was trying not to laugh.

"Too soon?" I asked, smiling.

He let out the laugh he was holding back, shaking his head. "No, I'm just glad you're able to joke about it."

By the end of lunch, I was back to fully relaxed and stuffed full of delicious food.

"I don't want to go back to work," I groaned, leaning back in my seat.

"Well today is an early day, isn't it? At least you're almost done," Lane pointed out.

"Very true. Which also means I need to get back there and finish up all my work, so I don't have to bring it home with me."

We stood up and left after paying. Lane stopped me outside my work building and pulled me into another hug, rubbing my back.

"I'm glad you came to lunch with me today," he said.

"I'm glad, too," I answered, pulling him in closer.

"Is it inappropriate if I kiss you in front of your work?" Lane asked, pulling back just enough to look me in the eyes, his manly scent invading my senses.

I closed my eyes and inhaled, enjoying it. "It might be, but I'm not sure I care right now," I whispered back.

Lane moved in and leaned his head to mine, meeting me halfway. Our lips met, melting me where I stood. Lane's hand supported my back, the other one against the back of my neck, holding me to him. I sighed, opening my mouth to his when his tongue swept across my lips. His greeted mine, swirling around each other.

My arms pulled him even closer, enjoying his tall frame pressed against me. I forgot where I was when I kissed him. My senses melded into one enjoyable feeling, not caring who was around. Happiness flooded through me as I stood there kissing Lane. Wanting to do more with Lane. Wishing we were back at my place.

I heard a cough nearby, and then a louder one. I pulled back from Lane and looked around to find Julie standing on the sidewalk gawking at us. My cheeks instantly flushed red and I stepped away from Lane to an acceptable distance. How embarrassing to be caught making out in public!

Julie's wide eyes seemed to be trying to communicate with me as she walked into the building, and I knew I was in trouble as soon as I got inside. I shuddered at the prospect of the rest of my day being filled with her wanting to gossip.

Lane took my hand, pulling me toward him for another hug and kiss before releasing me. "I'll let you get back to work before I get you into trouble."

"Too late for that. Julie is going to be upstairs waiting on me to fill her in on all the details," I groaned.

He laughed. "I would say I'm sorry, but I can't apologize for that kiss. It was, wow."

I smiled at him. "Okay, fine. Well I'll text you when I get home and we can get together. Sound good?"

He agreed and walked away to his car. I sighed with relief at how lunch had gone and then went inside, dreading Julie's assault.

Just as I suspected, Julie was lying in wait right outside of the elevator doors. She kept badgering me about whose "face I was sucking on" outside. Mortified, I quickly mumbled an explanation and made my way to my desk, trying to keep busy so she wouldn't pester me anymore.

By the end of work, I had managed to be so busy that I had completed all my work, plus some extra that I didn't even need to start yet. I got my desk organized, sorting my pens and markers by size and color, my office supplies back in their bins instead of being scattered around, and my phone and desktop had been wiped down of their dust and smudges. Satisfied, I glanced around to make sure Julie was occupied and then made my way out.

I drove home, finally feeling relaxed. Last night and today had taken a toll on me and I was ready for a nap. When I got home, I noticed Whitney had left a note on the fridge saying she was out for a run.

Perfect, I thought, stripping off my work clothes and putting on a pair of pajama shorts and a tank top. I went back to the living room and sprawled out on the couch, cocooning myself in the blanket we had laid on the back of it. This was my favorite nap spot in the apartment, even better than my bed. My bed was for real sleeping, but the couch was for quick and easy naps.

I felt my eyes growing heavier as I lied there, and finally succumbed to sleep. I woke up later to Whitney banging around in the kitchen and I groaned, stretching.

"Good evening, sleepyhead," I heard from the recliner.

I froze and then looked over. Lane was sitting there with a beer in his hand, watching me. Or more obviously, watching *all* of me. My blanket had slid down, and my tank top had shifted up, exposing my stomach.

I laid a hand on my stomach, Lane's eyes following my movement. I rubbed it lightly, arching my back a little more to stretch. "Well good evening to you, too," I said, smiling. "What brings you here?"

"Well, I did have an idea for plans, but I think I need to change them," he said, keeping an eye on my roaming hand. I lowered it to the waistband of my shorts, lightly stroking my stomach from left to right and back again.

"Oh yeah?" I feigned an interest in what Lane was saying as I rolled to my side to face him. "What plans?"

"Um, I'm not sure anymore," he said, rubbing a hand through his hair and shifting in his seat.

"What did you want to do instead?" I asked, narrowing my eyes at him.

Lane grinned at me. "Nothing that I want to do with Whitney being here too. So, we're out of luck on that one."

I stood up and bent down to retrieve the fallen blanket, knowing full well that I was giving Lane quite the show. I folded the blanket and laid it back down across the back of the couch and then turned to him. "I'm going to go get dressed."

"Do you have to?"

I smirked at him. "Well, you said we didn't really have any plans, so yeah. I think I'm going to go get dressed."

I went to my room and put on jeans and a t-shirt. Coming back out, I saw Lane was in the kitchen with Whitney and I went to join them.

"So, are we going out tonight or what?" Whitney asked as I sat down on a bar stool.

I looked at Lane, who shrugged. "I honestly didn't have any plans in mind. I just wanted to come over and hang out with you, since last night wasn't great," he said.

"To The Den?" I suggested, looking around at them. "Lane, what about your brother, is he doing anything?"

Lane took out his phone. "I'll call him real quick, see what he's up to."

After he left, Whitney turned to me. "Okay, spill. What happened at lunch?"

I smiled at her. "Well I told him I loved him."

Whitney squealed, clapping her hands. "Oh yay! Did he get down on his knees and beg forgiveness?"

I laughed. "No, he didn't! Geez! But he did apologize a lot, and seemed genuinely sorry, plus he sent those texts last night too. So, I've forgiven him and I'm moving forward."

Whitney came around the counter to hug me. "I'm happy for you. Really."

I hugged her close. "Thanks Whitney. He makes me really happy. How's Luke doing? Any luck there?"

Whitney gave me a knowing smile. "Definitely. I've got his phone number and we've been texting all day. Even at work, he kept sending me cute little messages and pictures."

My heart melted a little for her. It had been a long time since I had seen Whitney this happy because of a guy. Her last boyfriend had left her after confessing to cheating on her for over half of the year they had been dating. The devastation I witnessed was something I never wanted her to go through again.

"I'm happy for you too, Whitney! But you know I'll have to grill him when I meet him. I can't have anything but the best for you! Why don't you invite him out tonight?"

"I already did," she said, waving her phone around. "While you were knocked out on the couch snoring, I was getting a group night set up for us to go out."

I rolled my eyes. "I do *not* snore."

I felt hands on my shoulders. "Yeah, you do. It's cute though. Like a womanly snore."

I swatted my hand back behind me, hitting Lane. "Shut up. Even if I do snore, you're not supposed to tell me I do! And I don't snore. So, it doesn't matter."

Lane and Whitney exchanged glances before cracking up laughing. I stood up, a scowl on my face. "Fine, go ahead and laugh. I'm going to go get ready." I turned around and left to the bathroom to do my hair and makeup.

A couple hours later, the three of us plus Luke, Lane's brother Kent, Julie, and a few of our other co-workers were at The Den, drinking and exchanging funny work stories. I nudged Lane when I noticed Julie kept glancing over at Kent over her fruity cocktail. Lane watched her for a minute and smiled, leaning over to me.

"I'm not sure Kent is into the cougar type."

I hit his arm. "She's not that much older!" I looked back and forth between Kent and Julie. "Okay, so she is a bit older. Like twenty years older." I furrowed my brow, trying to decide what to do.

Lane turned my head to face him, leaning in toward me. "Relax, Abby. Whatever happens, happens. Don't worry about your friend or my brother. They're adults, so let them do what they want."

I nodded, knowing that was true. "I just don't want to see Julie get hurt. She can be annoying and over-the-top flirtatious, but she's really vulnerable and has horrible luck in dating."

Lane gave me a peck on the lips. "I love that you're protective of your friends. Even if they do annoy you."

I kissed Lane back. "Thanks for that. I love you, too."

His eyes lit up. "I'll never tire of hearing you say that."

I was about to respond when a wadded-up napkin hit the seat between us. I looked up at the group, ready to yell at whoever had ruined our moment. I noticed Whitney had that wide-eyed innocent look on her face and I glared at her. I grabbed the napkin and threw it back at her, hitting her in the chest. "Thanks a lot, Whit!"

She busted out laughing. "Sorry! Okay, not really, but you guys were getting too serious over there! This is supposed to be a fun night and we're out with all our friends! Come on!"

I rolled my eyes at her and stood up. "Fine! Shots for everyone!" I made my way over to the bar and ordered a round for our table.

As the hours passed, I felt myself relaxing more. I felt safe here, surrounded by my friends. By the time everyone was ready to leave, my head was buzzing and I was feeling loose-limbed. I had to grab onto Lane's arm to steady myself as we made our way out to the sidewalk where we said goodbye to some of our friends. Ten minutes later, it was just me, Lane, Whitney, and Kent left standing there.

"Well, doesn't this bring back memories," I said.

Whitney huffed. "Yeah, let's not bring *that* up right now. That wasn't that great of a night! You almost got ran over!"

I took a step toward her and stumbled. "Hey, hey, hey. I think it was a *fantastic* night. I did meet Lane, after all."

Lane smiled at me while holding my arm to keep me upright. "Very true. And if you're ready, we should probably get you ladies home."

The street swayed when I looked at it, causing my stomach to roll. "One of these days, I'm going to learn my lesson and not drink so much." I pressed a hand to my stomach to try to calm it.

We started across the street when the light turned green and I slowed down to walk with Whitney, wanting to talk to her about Luke. I had noticed that they seemed more intimate than I had thought they were, sharing heated looks and leaning over to whisper in each other's ears.

When we were almost to the other side, I heard a scream from behind me and turned to look back.

"No freakin' way," I whispered. "This can't be happening again."

A red four-door car was whipping around the corner, trying to beat the red light. Tires squealed as it raced down the street and all I could do was stand there and stare at it. It was coming closer as it turned onto the street we were crossing. The wind picked up, dragging my hair across my face as I stood in the path of the crazed driver.

It was as if I wasn't in control of myself, like I could only watch what was happening. I could hear Lane and Whitney yelling at me to move, but my body felt sluggish, as if it was weighed down. I turned my head to look at them, realizing that the whole world seemed to be in slow motion.

Then everything crashed down around me at once, time speeding back up. My arm was yanked to the side, forcing me out of the path of the car right as it drove past us. Screaming was all around me as I fell to the ground, Lane underneath me.

Whitney grabbed my other arm and pulled me up and onto the sidewalk, tears running down her face. "What the hell is wrong with you? Why didn't you move?"

I could only stare at her. My mind hadn't caught up with the events that had just happened, and I felt confused, like I wasn't sure of where I was or who I was with. My brain was filled with cotton and feeling fuzzy. I look at Lane and Kent, who were both staring at me like I had sprouted an extra eyeball.

I cleared my throat. "Um, I don't know. I guess I was scared and froze."

But I knew what happened. Deep down the truth was slowly creeping its way into my brain. This was no coincidence. Once, sure. Twice, maybe. Three times? No way. How could the same car keep coming around the corner every time we were here? No, not every time. It was Friday. I met Lane on a Friday night. When I tried to break up with him and came to The Den it was a Friday.

Friday nights at this exact corner, a red car came crashing around the corner every time I tried to cross the street. No, definitely not a coincidence. This was just more evidence to me, and this car was an important piece of the puzzle.

I thought back to the strange phone call I had heard from the dream during my migraine episode. *I suggest extreme actions.* Chills raced down my spine. *You need to kill that one.*

Oh, God. Was I the one that was meant to die?

Chapter Nine

I spent the rest of the weekend in bed. I couldn't force myself to get out. Whitney kept coming in to check on me, but I insisted that I was fine, just tired. And I was. So tired. I couldn't keep anything straight anymore.

My mind was running a million miles an hour. The car. The note. The dreams. The phone calls. The migraines. Everything pointed to either my insanity or that the note was real. But that pushed at the boundaries that my brain could handle.

I couldn't deal with this. Which was why I was staying in bed. I refused to move and make myself think more of what was going on.

Lane kept calling after he had dropped me off with Whitney on Friday night. I texted him once on Saturday to let him know I was feeling sick and couldn't meet up with him. It was just enough to get him to back off so I could wallow in self-pity.

What in the hell was wrong with me? I could feel the burn of tears as they blurred my vision again. I couldn't stop myself from crying, even though my eyes felt swollen and itchy. As soon as I thought I had calmed down, I would think about everything and then I would start crying all over again.

I had to figure this out. I had to get control of the situation so I could get back to normal. Maybe I should just commit myself and be done with it. I wasn't worth the trouble I was causing everyone. Whitney was giving me weird looks every time she came in to check on me and I knew Lane probably wasn't buying my excuses either.

I huffed and rolled over onto my back. I rubbed my eyes and took a few deep breaths to get control of myself. I had to get up so I could get ready for work, but I was starting to wonder what the point was. If I was in a dream, then why bother working? I didn't actually need the money. I didn't need to eat, I didn't need to work. I didn't need anything. I needed to wake up.

My eyes widened at that thought. It was the first time I had acknowledged that maybe I was really in a dream state and not going crazy. I sat up, pushing my hair back behind my ears. I felt a weight lift from my chest, like a relief was given to me that I hadn't realized I was needing. Now that I had made a decision on if what I was going through was real or fake, I felt like I could move forward. Figure this thing out. Even if it was just me alone doing it.

I couldn't imagine doing this alone though. Would Whitney and Lane really stay by my side if I told them I was sure this was all fake now? I could just see their anger now if I told them that I had made them up in my head.

I groaned and stood up, getting dressed for work. This was stressing me out. I wasn't ready to tell them. I would keep it to myself for now, at least until I had things worked out some more.

With that, I went out to the kitchen to grab a quick breakfast before I left. Whitney was already out there, sipping a cup of coffee while scrolling through her phone. She looked up when I walked in.

"Good morning," she said cautiously, watching me closely.

I smiled at her and got some juice out of the fridge. "Good morning," I said, closing the door and turning to her.

"Feeling better?"

I nodded, taking a drink. "Yeah, I am. All rested up and ready to get back into my work routine."

"Well, good," she said, standing up. "I'm going to get ready too."

I finished my juice and grabbed a banana and granola bar to take with me to eat on the car ride. Eating them on the way to work, I was feeling more relaxed than I had in a few weeks. There was no more reason to stress out.

I stopped halfway out of getting out of my car. Wait, there was a reason to be stressed. I had to figure out how to wake up. Oh geez. I sighed and gently banged my forehead on my steering wheel, praying for it to give me some ideas.

Making my way upstairs, I passed Julie sitting at her desk. She brightened when she saw me and got up, cornering me in the break room where I was headed.

"Abigail! What happened to you this weekend! I needed someone to gab with!"

I turned away from her and grimaced as I fixed myself a cup of coffee. Facing her again, I put a smile on my face. "What's up? What happened?"

Julie grinned, bouncing up and down on her toes. "I wanted to find out what was up with Lane's brother, Kent! Is he single, is he dating, does he like older women, what's the deal?" she spewed out without taking a breath.

I laughed despite my annoyance. This woman just didn't know when to stop. It was one of her character flaws, but at the same time made her a bit endearing. "As far as I know he's single. I have no idea what his type of woman is though."

She bit her lip, frowning. "I'm too old for him though. I know that. I guess it's stupid of me to even want to find out."

I reached out a hand to comfort her, sympathy causing me to be more patient than usual with her. "Hey, it's no problem here. It's easy enough to ask Lane for a few clues for you. And if he's seeing someone or not interested, then at least you know, right?"

Julie nodded. "Okay, you're right. Thanks a lot, Abigail!" She leaned in and hugged me, taking me off guard. I awkwardly patted her back, unused to this amount of interaction with her.

"Okay, I need to get to work," I said, taking a step back from her.

"Oh, of course! I need to as well. I've got a lot on my plate today."

I gave a sort of half-wave and headed back to my desk with my coffee. Sitting down, I turned on my computer and gave my desk a once-over, making sure everything was in order. Sipping my coffee, I pulled out the manuscripts I was working on and set them down, arranging them how I liked them.

The next few hours I found myself having to force my mind to the task at hand. I couldn't concentrate no matter how I tried. My thoughts kept going back to the red car that came to The Den's street corner every Friday. What was the point of that?

I tried to put myself out of my own mind and think outside the box. What was the significance of that car and that corner? I sank my head into my hands, trying to block out the noises of the office and my co-workers.

I jumped as something slammed onto my desk, barely keeping myself from yelling. I looked up and saw my manager, Lauren Cross, standing in front of me. She had slammed a thick book onto my desk.

"Sleeping on the job, Abigail?" she asked, crossing her arms as she stared down at me.

I sat up straight. "No, Lauren. Just sitting here thinking."

She narrowed her eyes at me. "Sure, okay. Just make sure you're thinking of work. And not anything else. You're here to work, not daydream." She grabbed her book, glared at me and walked off back to her office.

I looked over and saw Julie watching us. Her eyes were open wide and I could tell she wanted to come over and ask what was going on. I shook my head at her so she would stay at her desk. I didn't need to be getting in more trouble. Glancing over at Lauren's closed door, I couldn't help but wonder what the heck was wrong with her that she needed to come out and yell at me.

I sighed and turned back to my work, turning the pages until I found where I had left off. I was able to get work done for an hour or so, but then once again, the red car came back into my thoughts.

Crazy car. Friday nights. Same corner. I groaned quietly, not able to figure out the connections between the clues. What were they?

After lunch, I returned to my desk, determined to keep my focus on my work. It was almost time to go home for the day and I was happy I only had a couple more hours to power through before I could leave.

Suddenly, I remembered the drunken dream I'd had last Wednesday after drinking with my new medicine. I was standing in the street and Lane was trying to get to me before the car hit me. I thought back over the details as best as I could recall them. I hadn't been scared in the dream, in fact it had seemed like I was ready for the car to hit me.

I furrowed my brows in confusion. *It was just a dream*, I thought. But was it also a clue? I giggled at the thought of getting a Sherlock costume on and following a magnifying glass for more clues.

Okay, maybe I could work with this. I shot a look at Lauren's door, relieved that it was still closed. I didn't need to bring her wrath on me again. I got a piece of paper out of my notebook and wrote down the details of the dream. I wasn't sure if the street I had been standing in was the same one as where The Den was or if it was just a generic dream street, but I knew the car was important.

Okay, I thought, looking at the paper. *The car was going to hit me. I was going to let it. Lane tried to get me to safety. Well, that one is easy enough to figure out, of course he would want me to be safe.*

The car was going to hit me, and I was going to let it. I looked at those lines again. The car at The Den was close to hitting me each time it came by. What was the point of that? Was I supposed to let it? I shuddered at the thought of being hit by a car and hurt. No, I didn't want to do that.

So, what then? *Connect the dots, Abigail. Come on, figure this out. Figure it out!* I mentally shouted to myself. I tapped my pen on my forehead, hoping for some inspiration.

After a few minutes, I sat up, admitting defeat. I couldn't get it. What was so important about me and that car? My head was hurting from all this thinking I was doing, which was just sad. I got up to go to the break room to look for some Tylenol.

After sitting back down at my desk, I swallowed the pills down with some water. Luckily this was just a regular headache and not a migraine coming on. I didn't think I could handle another one of those just yet. Especially if I was thrust into another crazy dream while I was down.

I thought about my migraines and how they had only started five years ago. And the pain always originated on the left side of my head. *Another clue?* I laughed while I pictured myself twirling an impressive mustache at my potential find. Okay, okay, back to business.

So, if this was a dream state, what caused the coma? Could it have been the car? Maybe if a note had found its way into my dream, then other things could have as well. Like my migraines and the car. *Don't forget the hallucinations*, I thought wryly.

But, what if? I wondered, swinging my chair side to side. I flipped my paper over and started a new list. The car could have caused the coma and my migraines. Or maybe I hit my head and that's why I get my migraines. I wasn't sure that it even mattered. If I was in a dream, then I shouldn't even be feeling pain. Isn't that the first thing people check when they think they're dreaming? They pinch themselves.

I tried it and felt the sharp pain as I clamped down on my skin. Well, that part didn't add up.

Hearing people walking toward the desks, I quickly shoved the paper into my purse and sat back up, pretending to be reading and making notes. I just couldn't concentrate, and I wasn't even feeling guilty about it. I felt disconnected from what I was doing. Nothing mattered anymore except figuring out what was going on.

I pretended to work the rest of the day, while I pondered on the list in my purse. I was itching to get it back out and work on it, but Lauren was stalking around the office area, making sure we were all doing our work.

I was the first one to shoot out of my chair at the end of the day, speed-walking to the door with my purse hanging from my hand. I needed to get home and make sure I was getting the right answers.

Walking into the apartment, I was glad to see Whitney wasn't home yet. I did not need her here to witness my potential downfall into insanity, in case I was wrong about all of this.

Reading over my notes, I noticed again the pattern that had emerged. The car, the street corner, every Friday night I was there. I wondered if the car was there every Friday night or if it only showed up when I was there. "Too bad I can't put up secret cameras to see," I mused.

After a while I sat back, examining my work. I wasn't sure if I had figured it out, but my best guess was that the car had caused the coma, and that was why I was seeing it here. That had to be why it was always so close to hitting me here. I had been hit by a car, probably thrown, hit my head and now here I was. Living a fake life with a fake job, fake friends, and a fake boyfriend. My heart wrenched at that thought, the pain almost too much to bear.

Even if I managed to wake up, I couldn't imagine a life without Lane in it. I had come to rely on him so much and the support and love that he gave me. I didn't want to give that up, but I couldn't keep going on like this either. I needed to wake up more than I wanted to stay here. The guilt I felt at that thought flooded through me, my face burning with shame and tears filling my eyes.

I took a shaky breath and kept the tears at bay, not wanting to cry anymore. I had done enough of that the past month or so. Standing up, I pushed my shoulders back and went to the bathroom to clean up. I didn't want Whitney to know I was upset when she came home.

Going back to the living room, I paced back and forth in front of the couch. "The car caused the coma. It hit me, I hit the ground, so here I am. So how do I wake up? How do I wake up? The note said it was a new technology and that's how it got into this dream world. Okay, so why can't that technology wake me up?" I growled as I threw my hands up in frustration. "Why am I the one doing all the hard work?"

I thought about my parents out in the real world, waiting on me to open my eyes. What were they doing? Were they just hanging out in my hospital room, watching me waste away? It had been five years, according to the note. I was sure I was looking like a hot mess at this point.

"If the car caused the coma, maybe it could *un-cause* it?" I wondered, feeling the blood leave my head, causing a dizzy feeling to spread. "What if the only way is to get hit by the car again? Ugh, but so many things could go wrong!" I started to pace again.

"What if it didn't hit me at all, or what if it doesn't hit me the right way? Maybe I'll just break an arm and not wake up." I rubbed at my temples as I walked around.

I straightened up and stood still. "No, this is the only thing that makes sense. The car has to be the key to this, so the car is going to be the way to fix this. Then I can wake up…and lose everything." I faltered at that, then shook my head. "No, no, I have to do this."

What's the next step, then? If I was really going to do this, then I wanted to get everything straightened out here that I could. I wasn't sure that made much sense, since I had decided that this was all a fake world I was in, but my brain could only handle so much at one time.

I gathered up my papers and put them back in my purse, hiding it in my room. I knew Whitney wouldn't go through my things, but I didn't want to chance it either. After that was done, I went into the kitchen and started making dinner, trying to keep a semblance of normalcy.

Whitney arrived right as I was taking the casserole out of the oven. I looked over at her and smiled. "Hey there. How was work?"

Whitney smiled and sat down on a stool. "Man, I'm worn out. Today was just busy, busy, busy and there was no slowing down. How about you?"

I turned away from her. "Oh, it was all right. My boss was on our asses a lot today. Not sure what her problem was."

Whitney scrunched her nose. "Ugh, that sucks. Bosses should just stay in their office and do what they do from there."

"I totally agree. She was making everyone nervous today."

"What else have you been up to? Is Lane coming over tonight?" she asked.

I shook my head. "No, I don't think so. I haven't talked to him today."

Whitney looked over, a weird look on her face. "Really? You didn't see him all weekend. I figured you would be seeing him tonight."

"Nope. I'm just hanging out here tonight."

Whitney didn't say anything to that, and I didn't turn around to look at her. I didn't want her to try to read the emotions on my face after my revelation earlier. I didn't want to see her look of betrayal and pain after I told her I was sure she was a figment of my imagination.

So instead I stayed in denial and kept my back turned. Getting out the plates, I fixed them up with the casserole I had made and set them on the table. Then after getting our drinks, I sat down with those too.

Whitney kept a close watch on me, eyes narrowed in suspicion. I just ignored her and kept my eyes down, shoveling my food in my mouth so I could finish faster and be gone.

"Why aren't you seeing Lane? Did you guys get in a fight?"

I sighed and shook my head. "No, we didn't. I was just busy today at work and never got a chance to talk to him. It happens, you know."

Whitney tilted her head, pointing her fork at me. "Something's going on with you. What is it? I've never heard you give an excuse for not talking to Lane. You two are practically joined at the hip."

Shrugging, I took a bite of food. "Nothing's going on with us. I'm fine."

Whitney pursed her lips, obviously not believing me. I breathed a sigh of relief when she sat back, backing off from the questions. I stood up, grabbed my plate, and headed into the kitchen to rinse it off. Then I headed back to my room to deal with my papers I had stashed away.

****

The next day at work, I sat at my desk, taking deep breaths. I felt out of my depth here and more nervous than when I had interviewed for the job. I was basically throwing it back in my boss' face after she had gone through the trouble of hiring me over others that had more qualifications.

I looked over the letter in my hands again. I had spent a few hours last night writing my resignation, trying to perfect it before giving it to Lauren today. I couldn't keep up the façade of this life when I was convinced it wasn't real. I was ready to try to get out.

I stood up but lost my nerve when I looked at Lauren's closed door. *I need a drink*, I thought, wishing I could do exactly that. Instead, I went to the break room and made a cup of coffee, telling myself that it was something stronger.

Fortified, I strode to Lauren's door and knocked. When she answered, I opened the door and went in, shutting it behind me. I nervously sat down and waited for her to acknowledge me.

"What's up, Abigail?" she asked, typing on her computer without looking at me.

I fidgeted, trying not to wrinkle the letter I had in my hands. I held it out to her, wishing she would look at me.

"I have this for you. It's my resignation," I finally said, laying it on the desk.

That finally got Lauren to look at me, surprise on her face. "Resignation? How come? Did you get another job offer?"

I shook my head. "No. It's just, I have some things I need to do, some family things I need to help with. I can't work here and do those things too." There was no way to explain that I was dreaming all of this.

Lauren wrinkled her brows in confusion. "I don't understand. You can't work here while you deal with your family?"

"No, I can't. So, I'm giving you my resignation. I wouldn't want to do any subpar work while I was doing this." I stood up to leave, not wanting to draw this out any longer than I had to.

Lauren looked over the letter and then back at me. "Really, Abigail, you're not even giving me a proper two weeks' notice? That is highly unprofessional of you. I'm not sure that I can give you a good recommendation if your next job comes calling here about you."

I shrugged, feeling a weight lift off my shoulders. "That's okay. I won't be needing one anyway."

Lauren bristled. "Well then, feel free to go ahead and leave now and not finish out the workday. Bring all the manuscripts you were working on in here and leave them on my desk. I'll have to divvy them out amongst the others and give them even more work than they already have."

Trying not to let the guilt eat away at me, I walked to the door. "Thank you for everything, Lauren. I really do appreciate the opportunity I had here."

She just stared at me as I shut the door behind me, and I went back to my desk. I spent the next hour cleaning up my desk area and organizing my work and making notes on each manuscript on what I had done and where I had left off. Not that I thought Lauren would let my work stand anymore. She would probably have the others start completely over since I'm sure she thought I was incompetent now.

After leaving my work in Lauren's office, I gathered up my things and left. Luckily, it was lunch time, so nobody was in the office as I went. I didn't want to have any conversations with anyone about what I was doing and where I was going.

I stepped outside and took a deep breath, feeling relieved. *It's going to be okay*, I reassured myself. This was the first step I had to take to get back to my old life.

I went home and put on my comfortable clothes, yoga pants and a tank top. Putting on some music, I spent the next hour dancing around the apartment and letting the stress slough off me. It was only when I heard my phone ringing that I finally shut the music off.

"Hello?" I asked, out of breath.

"Abby? What's going on?" It was Lane.

"Oh, hey Lane," I answered, feeling a little unsure. I hadn't decided what to do about Lane yet, if I should keep him around or let him go before I got even more attached than I already was. I was going to be leaving all of this soon anyway.

"Are you not at work right now?" he asked.

"No, um, I'm not. I actually quit."

There was a moment of silence. "You quit? Why?"

I shrugged, even though I knew he couldn't see it. "I just didn't want to do it anymore."

More silence. "Abby, what's going on? You can't just quit your job," he said tersely.

"Sure I can. I just did."

"Can I come over?" I could just imagine him rubbing his hand through his hair in frustration.

"If you want to, sure," I answered.

"Okay. I'll be over in an hour or so, all right?"

"Sounds good to me. Bring some drinks over with you."

Lane sighed loudly. "Sure, Abby. I can do that."

After hanging up, I crossed to the fridge to see what we had in terms of snacks. Nothing that I wanted. So I looked up the number for a pizza delivery and ordered two larges. If Lane was coming over then I was sure that he could probably eat a whole one by himself.

It was almost exactly an hour later when I heard a key in the lock. The pizza had been delivered about twenty minutes before, so I was busy shoving a bite in my mouth when I turned around to the door. Whitney stood there with Lane at her side. In my surprise, I inhaled and started choking. They both came in and Lane started patting me on the back, easing my coughing.

"What are you doing here, Whitney? Shouldn't you be at work?" I asked her.

She crossed her arms and looked at me indignantly. "Shouldn't *you*?" she countered.

I raised my eyebrows before turning to Lane. "You told her? Seriously?"

"Yes, seriously. What is going on with you?" he asked.

I threw up my hands, huffing. "Nothing is going on! Can't a girl quit her job without anything being wrong?"

"Um, no, they can't," Whitney said. She sat on the couch and looked at me. "Tell us what's going on."

This was it. I had to tell them. I sat in the recliner as Lane sat on the couch. Two against one, or at least that's what it felt like. "Nothing is going on, really, I just, I, oh hell how do I say this?" I said to myself.

Lane reached over and grabbed my hand, rubbing his thumb across the back of it. "Whatever it is, it's okay."

I shook my head. "It's not going to be okay for you. I've been thinking. And, um, I'm starting to believe the note is true. It's true, okay? I'm convinced."

Neither Whitney nor Lane said anything, both staring at me with astonished looks on their faces. Then they both started talking at once.

"What the *hell*, Abigail!"

"Abby, you can't be serious!"

I held up my hands to get them to stop talking. "I am serious. There are just too many things that are starting to seem too coincidental that I can't ignore anymore. The doctors couldn't find anything on my tests, yet I'm hallucinating. I've almost been hit by a car three times now. *Three!* At the same time and place every time! I'm having the weirdest dreams during my migraines. There's just too much to write off."

Lane was shaking his head while Whitney just gaped at me. She stood up, muttering, "I need a drink," and walked off to the kitchen.

I looked back at Lane, who just kept staring at me. The concern on his face was touching, but I didn't want him to keep worrying about me. I knelt on my knees in front of him. "Please, don't worry about me. I'm okay, really."

He didn't look convinced. "Abby, this is just crazy. You can't really think this, can you?"

I nodded. "Yeah, I can. And I do."

He leaned forward, a hand on either side of my face. "You think this isn't real?" he whispered. "That I'm not real?"

Tears sprang to my eyes and I blinked them away. "You're as real to me as you can be. Which is only as real as I make you. I hate that I'm hurting you, and Whitney too, but Lane, I need out. I need to get out of my head. Back to the real world."

He leaned back, hurt on his face. "As real as you make me? You think you've just made me up? That my whole life is some product of your imagination? You're a smart girl Abby, but you're not acting like it right now."

That stung. "You don't have to sit here and take jabs at me, Lane. It's not necessary."

"Then just imagine me away, Abby. Since apparently that's all I am to you."

I sat back on my heels. "You mean everything to me Lane, and you know it. I love you."

He shook his head. "How can you love something that you've made up?"

"I just can, I guess." I gave him a small smile, hoping it would lighten him up.

Whitney came back in and sat down again with her drink. "Okay. You need help Abigail. Help that we can't give you here."

I got up and sat back in the recliner. "I don't need a therapist, Whitney. I'm fine."

"You're not fine. You're so stuck in your head that you think you really are *stuck in your head.*"

"Good one, Whitney," I said flatly. "Not amused."

"Good, Abigail. I'm not trying to be amusing."

"Look guys, nothing is wrong. I'm fine. Actually, I feel better than I have since I got that stupid note. I feel like I'm finally going in the right direction."

Whitney and Lane exchanged a glance, something going back and forth between the two of them. After a minute, they finally looked back at me.

Whitney leaned forward. "Abigail, we both love you. We want what's best for you. And you're not, this isn't…" She couldn't finish though, and sat back, wiping tears from her face.

Lane patted her knee, comforting her. "It's okay, Whitney. Abby, we're concerned about you. What you're saying just isn't sane."

"You think I'm crazy?" I asked, looking back and forth between the two of them. Taking a deep breath, I nodded. "Okay, okay, I can see that. But I'm not crazy, you two. I've spent so long thinking this over, and it's the only logical conclusion I can come to."

"The only *logical* conclusion?" Lane asked. "There's nothing logical about what you're saying."

Whitney gestured at me. "I've already had this conversation with her. I've told her that I am *not* made up. I'm *not!*"

I started crying again. "Why can't you guys just see where I'm coming from here? You think this is so easy for me? Maybe you two could try experiencing what I've been going through for the last month or so and then you can tell me how you two feel about it. It's not fair for you two to just sit there and judge me on this when you have no idea what it is I'm going through!"

I felt more anger coursing through me than I ever had before. The strength of it surprised me as it caused me to say things I normally wouldn't otherwise.

"Screw both of you. Thanks so much for your support," I spat out, standing and going into the kitchen. I paced back and forth, wiping tears away as they slid down my cheeks.

After a few minutes, I heard someone enter behind me. I kept my back turned away stubbornly. Arms wrapped around me, holding me against a firm chest I knew was Lane's. He settled his chin on the top of my head, his breaths settling me, the anger and hurt easing out of me.

We stayed like that for a while, me leaning against Lane. I turned around and nestled my head into his chest. "I hate fighting," I whispered to him.

He leaned down and kissed the top of my head softly. "I do, too," he whispered back. "I don't want us to be like this."

I sighed. "I don't either. But I'm not changing my mind about anything, either."

Lane's arms tightened around me. "I won't say that I agree with you. I don't think I can, not now or...well, I just can't. Is that going to be okay?"

I nodded. "It'll be okay. I guess we'll just have to avoid talking about this then."

"I think I can handle that," Lane said, his hands rubbing up and down my back.

I reached up, kissing his neck, feeling the stubble on his chin graze across my cheek. I leaned up further and kissed his lips, feeling them soft yet firm against mine. "We could really just not talk at all," I suggested.

Lane smiled against my lips, kissing them one last time before moving away. "I think that's a fantastic idea, but Whitney probably wouldn't appreciate it. I think she's waiting to talk to you, actually."

Groaning, I leaned my forehead against his chest. "I know, I know. I do need to talk to her. But it's not going to go well. I can't get her to stop talking by kissing her."

Lane's eyes glittered with amusement when he looked down at me. "You can't?"

I laughed, slapping at his chest. "No, I can't, you Neanderthal. Okay, I guess I'll go in there."

Lane slapped me on the butt as I passed him. "Go get her, tiger."

I rolled my eyes at him and left to go talk to Whitney. She was sitting on the couch where I had left her, drinking her wine. I sat next to her, waiting for her to acknowledge that I was there.

"Whitney, don't hate me."

"Is that what you think? I don't hate you, Abigail. But what in the world are you thinking?" she asked, looking up at me.

I just looked at her. "Haven't you ever believed something that nobody else did? This is that for me. Nobody believes me. They don't believe I'm experiencing what I say I am, nobody can see that note, except for Lane for whatever weird reason. It's all just too much! So, I'm trying to face it head on and figure it out. And if that means that this whole thing isn't real, that I'm just dreaming this, then that's what I have to do."

Whitney shook her head at me. "I can't agree with this. I've told you this before, and I'm telling you again. I'm not made up. I'm not a figment of your imagination that you created. Everything in this world is too complex for you to have thought up. You have to admit that. You can't have done all of this."

Disappointment was all I felt as I listened to what Whitney said. She was my best friend and I had hoped that she would be on my side, but I guess that was too much to hope for.

"I'm going to say what I said to Lane. We'll just have to agree to not talk about this. There's no way for us to agree on this topic, and neither of us is changing our minds about it."

Whitney opened her mouth to argue, but I spoke first. "Please, Whitney. I don't want to lose you as a friend."

She narrowed her eyes at me and stood up. "According to you, I'm not real. So just go ahead and use your imagination and pretend that I'm your friend still. That should work for you, shouldn't it?" She walked away, and I heard her door slam a moment later.

I couldn't move from my seat. Five years of friendship was gone. I was too stunned for tears to even appear. Taking a deep breath, I stood up and saw Lane in the doorway to the kitchen.

"You heard that?" I asked.

He nodded. "Yeah. I'm sorry, Abby."

I looked down. "I didn't think she would react like that. I thought we could just agree to disagree about it. What am I going to do without her now?"

Lane walked over to me and gathered me into a hug, holding me tightly. "I love you, Abby. We'll figure this out together, okay?"

"Okay," I said, breathing him in.

We stood there for a few minutes, slightly swaying back and forth. My mind was whirring with too much information and thinking about what to do next. In my heart I knew that there was no point in delaying the next part of my plan.

Chapter Ten

The next morning, I woke up and just relaxed in bed for a while. It felt weird not having to get up for work and I had almost panicked when I saw the time and thought I was going to be late. Lane had stayed for a few hours last night, and if I were honest with myself, he had me feeling more relaxed than I had been in half a week. The stress of the weekend, work, and the note all but disappeared while Lane was with me.

Sighing, I sat up, running my fingers through my hair. I had a few days until Friday came by, which is the next time I would see the car. The thought of what I was planning to do was making me nauseous enough that I had to straighten up and take some deep breaths before I made a mess of my bed.

Getting up, I took a few minutes to straighten my room up and get dressed. There was something freeing in knowing that I didn't have to be anywhere. I had no schedule to follow and I could just do whatever I wanted.

Feeling a little better, I made my way downstairs and went to a café a few blocks away. I had brought a book with me and read it while I munched on a breakfast sandwich and drank some coffee. I wished I could do this all day, every day. It was so relaxing that I stayed there for two more hours, just huddled in my chair and listening to the background noise of the other customers going about their day.

By the time my stomach started rumbling for lunch, I had finished my book. When was the last time I was able to read a book and it not be for work? I wasn't used to being able to just read whatever and whenever I wanted to, but I didn't want it to stop. My dream world should be about what I wanted to do, and I had three more days to enjoy it.

I got up and went back to the apartment and grabbed my car keys. I spent the rest of the day driving around with the windows down and stopping whenever I felt like it to window shop or grab a snack to eat. It was the freest I had probably ever felt, and I never wanted it to end.

That thought sobered me up. I found it pretty ironic that I was feeling this way only to know that

none of it was real and that I was about to end it soon.
And I still had no way of knowing whether I was
right or wrong about my theory. That probably
scared me the most. Was I about to make the worst
mistake of my life? Was I about to throw it all away
on a hunch? Whitney's words resonated with me and
I couldn't help the sliver of doubt that crept through
my mind.

Shaking my head, I headed back to the
apartment. It was time to figure out my actual plan. I
wasn't sure that I could just wing it and be okay with
that. I didn't want to mess anything up, and I
definitely did not want to drag anybody else into it
with me. I needed to do this on my own. Lane and
Whitney shouldn't have to watch me throw myself in
front of a car, not knowing what the outcome would
be.

Whitney was still gone when I went inside.
She wasn't talking to me, which hurt more than I
wanted to think about. She may not agree with me,
and I couldn't blame her for that, but she was
throwing away five years of friendship. My best
friend. Gone in the blink of an eye, without an ounce
of remorse. I didn't want to leave on Friday and not
say goodbye to her.

I went to my room and grabbed a pad of paper
and a pen. Sitting at my desk, I pushed aside all my
other notes from work and random things that I had
dropped down and never put away in their proper

place. Chewing on the pen cap, I thought about what I wanted to say.

Whitney,

I'm not sure how to put down the words that I want to say here. You've been my best friend for so long, that I don't know what I would do without you. I don't think that I'll ever get you to understand what I'm going through right now. And that's okay. It's my struggle to get through and you shouldn't have to worry about me. I know you don't agree with me, but I never thought that you would turn against me either. How am I supposed to be okay with you being so mad at me? You've always been there for me, just like I have for you. But now you're not. If our roles were reversed, I know that I would support you in whatever decision you would make. But the second that things got hard and I decided to go down a different path that you didn't like, you just turned your back and abandoned me. Even Lane didn't do that. He's sticking by me, like you should be doing. I'm sorry that we're at this place, and I know it's my fault. But I'm hurting right now, and you don't even see it.

I'm going to miss you when I'm gone. You truly are my best friend and I'll never forget the amazing times that we've had over the years.

Don't come looking for me.

I love you,

Abigail

I read over my note a few times until I decided that it was good enough. I grabbed an envelope out of my desk drawer and sealed it inside. I sat there for a few minutes, my heart feeling heavy in my chest. Then I straightened up, determined not to think about it anymore. I could do this. I had to. I hid the envelope in my desk drawer, saving it for Friday night when I would leave it out for Whitney to find when she got home from work. Until then, I would try to talk to her and hope that she answered me.

That night I was out in the living room watching television when I heard the door unlock and open. Whitney came in, talking on her phone. When she saw me sitting on the couch, she narrowed her eyes and went into her room, shutting the door behind her. I didn't expect to feel so hurt by that small action, but I was. I didn't know what the best thing to do was to solve this problem.

Sighing, I picked up my own phone, texting Lane. I felt bad about ignoring him over the weekend.

Me: *Hey, you busy?*

Lane: *No, I'm not. What's up?*

I cocked my head, trying to figure out what tone the text was sent in. I couldn't tell if he was really mad at me or just didn't care anymore. Or maybe I was reading too much into it.

Me: *Just wanting some company*

Lane: *I can be there in twenty minutes*

Me: *That's perfect*

I started to set my phone down but then brought it back.

Me: *I really miss you*

Lane: *I miss you too Abby. This weekend has been hell without you*

I smiled softly at that, feeling happy butterflies in my stomach at his words. At least I had Lane, even if only for a few more days. The smile slipped from my face. Just a few more days. That's all I had with him. I pushed the thought out of my mind, not wanting to start crying. I got up and started picking up in the living room, straightening things out to tidy up the place for when Lane arrived.

Going into the kitchen, I took a beer out of the fridge, hoping to calm my nerves. There was no reason to be nervous about Lane coming over, but we hadn't spoken since that I had told him I believed in the note. Ignoring his phone calls and messages had been a lot easier than talking to him about it.

Right on cue, there was a knocking on the front door. I went and opened it, feeling a flutter inside as I looked up at Lane. Not seeing him over the weekend, and only for a short while last night, had seemed to make him even more handsome than I remembered him to be. He had a shadow of growth on his face, giving him a rough look that I found incredibly sexy.

I moved my hand without realizing it, softly rubbing it against his beard. "I like this," I murmured.

He covered my hand with his own. "That's good. The last few days have been…rough, and I didn't feel up to the task of shaving it off."

I frowned. "I'm sorry, Lane. I'm a terrible person."

He smiled, shaking his head. "No, you're not. You're just going through a stressful time. It'll be okay. *We* will be okay."

I think I gave some semblance to a smile, because Lane relaxed. No need to inform him of my plan. He would only talk me out of it and try to stop me. The realization that I only had three more days with Lane depressed me more than I wanted to think about.

I stepped back so Lane could come inside. We went to the living room and sat down.

"Can I get you a drink or something?" I offered.

"Sure, I'll take a beer if you have one."

Nodding, I got up and went to grab him one. Popping the cap off, I brought it back and handed it to him. Then I sat down next to him, feeling the awkwardness of having not seen him in days coming at me.

Whitney opened her door and stepped out. She stopped when she saw us sitting there and I could see her practically rolling her eyes at us. I narrowed my eyes back at her, tired of the hostility I could feel pouring off her.

Lane looked back and forth between us before clearing his throat. "Hey, Whitney. How are you?"

Whitney tossed her hair back and looked at Lane. "I'm fine. How are you?"

Lane's face was starting to flush. "Um, I'm good, thanks. Do you want to join us?"

Whitney shook her head and looked at me. "No thanks. I'm good in my room, by myself." With that, she turned around and shut her door harder than necessary.

Lane looked between me and Whitney's door a few times before turning to me. "Have you guys not talked since last week?"

I shook my head. "No. I've tried a few times, but she's not having any of it. She just doesn't want to talk to me and she keeps blowing me off." I blinked away a few tears that were threatening to fall, not wanting to go down that path. "Five years of friendship is gone. She's my best friend and she won't be there for me now."

Lane scooted closer and gathered me in his arms, hugging me to him tightly. "Hey, it's okay. I know it's hard, but she's going to come around. Maybe not soon, but eventually she's going to stop being hurt over this and be your friend again."

I sighed, loving the reassurance even though I knew that there wouldn't be time for Whitney to get over her anger.

As if she could hear us talking about her, Whitney opened her door and came out, purse in hand.

"You going out?" I asked, trying to be friendly.

"Yup."

I looked at Lane, and he nodded at me to keep trying.

"You want company?"

"No," came the short reply.

My frustration was almost to a breaking point, so I decided to cut it short and let her go. "Well, have fun I guess."

"Thanks." With that, Whitney walked out the door, slamming it shut.

"God, she hates me," I said, rubbing my hands over my face.

"No, she doesn't. She doesn't understand what you're going through right now and that you need her friendship more than ever. She'll come around. Don't worry about it."

I leaned over to hug him again, rubbing his back with my hands. The feeling of his muscles was enough to relax me and make me believe him. I adjusted my position until my face was leaning into his neck. Breathing deeply, I inhaled Lane's scent again, loving the manly smell that was mixed with his laundry detergent and body wash. I kissed there, wanting him to know how much I appreciated his strength and commitment.

Lane breathed in harshly, before turning his head to cover my mouth with his. His kiss pulled me under, sending me into a place of ecstasy that I hadn't experienced before. I drew back to look at him. He had a look of desire smoldering in his eyes, and I'm sure that it was mirrored in mine. I was breathing heavily and then I crashed into him like a wave kissing the beach, desperate for more. I pushed him back onto the couch and straddled him, laying on top of his chest. My heart hammered in my chest, resounding in my ears.

Lane moaned, and I could feel the air brush over my lips. His hands wandered greedily over my back and thighs. I reached under his shirt and feathered my hands over the muscles of his stomach, feeling them jump beneath my touch. I smiled against Lane's mouth, enjoying the effect that I had on him. In fact, I could *feel* the effect I had on him pressing into me.

My hands reached for the buttons of his shirt, undoing them as they made their way down to his waist. I skimmed the boundary that his jeans made, just barely reaching my fingertips inside them, sliding them left and right. Lane's hips bucked a little under me, pushing me forward onto him more.

Faster than I could think, Lane had us flipped over, my legs wrapped around his waist. I gasped, and Lane pushed his tongue toward mine, tangling them together in a dance. I wrapped my arms around him and pulled him in closer, wanting every gap between us to be filled. Lane pulled me up, lifting me against him as he stood up. I wrapped my legs around his waist and kissed up and down his neck, not wanting to break the connection we had.

He brought me to my room, laying me down on my bed. He kicked the door shut and collapsed down on top of me. I pushed his shirt down his arms while he tugged mine up and off. Lying there panting, I stared at him while he gazed back. Smiling, I ran a finger from his chest down his stomach, stopping at the button on his jeans.

"Are you sure about this?" he asked.

I nodded, biting my lip. "I am if you are."

He groaned and drew me in closer. "I've wanted you for a long time now, but I'll wait until you're ready."

I breathily answered him in-between kisses. "Yes. I'm sure. I want this, Lane."

Our pants disappeared quickly after that, leaving us in our underwear, hands wandering over previously forbidden territory. My heart was beating quickly, excitement quickening my breathing as I kissed Lane, my hands roaming south toward his boxer briefs.

I gripped him through the front of his underwear, relishing his gasp as he thrusted into my hand. He rolled me over so he was on top of me and unhooked my bra, dragging it down my arms and throwing it carelessly on the floor. Drawing back, he looked down, taking in his first sight of me, almost at my most vulnerable. I was tempted to cover myself up, growing shy under his adoring gaze, but I managed to keep my hands down.

Lane looked at me and smiled, leaning down to kiss me. "You're beautiful," he whispered.

I smiled, kissing him back. "So are you."

I pushed his boxers down, using my feet as they lowered around his knees. Lane followed suit, hands cupping my ass before he pulled my underwear off. I lifted my hips and pressed them into Lane's, taking pleasure in the warmth as our bodies touched. Moaning, I brought his head down to kiss him again.

Lane moved down, trailing kisses down my neck to my chest, reaching my breasts. He cupped them in his hands, bringing them together to kiss them, drawing my nipples into his mouth. I gasped, arching my back toward him. I grabbed his head, keeping him where he was, not wanting him to stop.

Lane laughed softly and kept going down to my stomach and then to my waist. He scooted down, bringing his mouth to my thighs, licking and sucking as he moved higher to reach my center. He kissed me there and I let out an explosive breath, delighting in Lane's mouth showing me just how talented he was.

A tingling started low down, building up inside me before I gave into it and cried out, grasping Lane's hair to hold him in place. As I came down from my high, I looked down and saw Lane grinning at me.

"Wow," was all I could manage.

"*You* are wow," he said, climbing back up to be face-to-face with me.

We kissed a moment longer before I wrapped my legs back around his waist, feeling his erection pressing against my center. I rubbed back and forth, feeling the tip of him against me. Lane reached down to the floor for his jeans and grabbed a condom out of his wallet. When I arched an eyebrow at him, he smiled at me and said, "Just in case. I like to be prepared."

He rolled the condom on and laid back down over me. Pushing into me, we both groaned at the contact, savoring the feeling of the deeper connection we had just made. The fullness made me feel complete and I relished in it. Finally, Lane pulled out and started moving into me again.

We breathed together, faces side by side, kissing when we had the chance. Lane moved his head down and nibbled on my neck, thrusting faster and faster. I felt the familiar sparks building again as he reached a spot inside me that I hadn't yet discovered.

Lane reached down and grabbed my hips, tilting them up. I cried out as he hit that delicious spot inside, drawing my climax out of me. Lane brought his head down, kissing me as he groaned and then stilled inside me. We lied there for a few minutes, gasping for air.

I turned my head and smiled at Lane. "That...was...wow," I said, still trying to catch my breath.

Lane rolled over, pulling out of me. I got up and grabbed a towel for us to clean off with and got back into my clothes. Lane did the same and then came over and pulled me in for a hug. I sighed, relaxing into him, wishing I could stay here forever.

You could *stay here forever,* I thought to myself. *Just don't go through with your stupid plan on Friday and you could be here with Lane having amazing sex every night.*

I pulled back, feeling guilty for not telling Lane what I was going to do. I looked up at him, smiling. "That was better than I had imagined."

He chuckled, rubbing his nose on mine. "I sure hope so. I love thinking about how you were imagining it though."

I playfully pushed him and laughed. "Stop! There was no 'imagining' going on!"

Lane laughed. "Okay, okay. Are you ready to get some dinner?"

"Yes! I'm starving! What do you have in mind?"

"How about some Chinese? I'm in the mood for some eggrolls."

I grabbed my purse off my desk. "Sounds delicious. Let's go."

****

After dinner, Lane decided to stay the night. I still hadn't seen Whitney since she had left earlier. I wasn't even sure if she had come back or not.

I flopped down onto the couch, wishing I could pull my pants down and let my belly hang out from all the food I had eaten. But I knew with Lane there that I couldn't do it. He might have seen me naked now, but there were still boundaries that I wasn't ready to cross.

Lane sat next to me, pulling me in close. Leaning down, he kissed the top of my head.

I sighed, almost feeling like the world was complete. Almost. If only I could forget that my world had turned upside down.

Right as I was about to say something, I heard keys jingling in the front door. Sitting up straight, I turned to look as Whitney came inside. She looked over at us and rolled her eyes, going into the kitchen.

Looking at Lane, I wondered what I should do. He smiled, understanding in his eyes. "Go to her. Make her talk to you."

I nodded, standing up. I could do this. I could *do this*. Shaking my hands to get the nerves out, I entered the kitchen. Whitney was leaning up against the counter, eating leftovers out of the container.

"Hi," I said softly.

Whitney didn't say anything, only putting more food into her mouth.

"Look, I want to talk to you. Please."

Huffing, Whitney looked up at me. "There's nothing to talk about."

"Yes, there is! You're my best friend and we haven't talked in days! Why? Because we disagree on something? Because my world is falling apart around me, and you can't support me in my decisions?" I started yelling, waving my hands around to emphasize the point.

Whitney pointed a finger at me. "Because you are not okay, Abigail. You are going completely insane, and you need help! If your little boyfriend out there isn't going to help you, then someone needs to."

I could feel my mouth gaping as I stared at her. "I am fine, Whitney. Just because I have been having problems lately does not mean that I'm going insane. I'm doing the best that I can."

She shook her head. "You are falling down the rabbit hole, Abigail. You are so far down there that you don't even realize you're there anymore."

My anger was dissipating, turning into calmness that flowed through me. "There is no rabbit hole, Whitney. All I need is for my friend to stand by my side. To support me in whatever decisions I make!"

"Oh, so if I made the decision to sleep with Lane, you would support me in that?" Whitney sneered at me. "Because, you know, that's what friends do. They support decisions that are being made."

I reached out before I could even think what I was doing and slapped Whitney, her face whipping to the side from the force. I gasped and took a step back, cradling my hand. Lane rushed in and stood between us, hands spread as if he was going to hold us apart from each other.

"Whitney, I'm so sorry," I whispered.

She held her cheek, the flaming red blooming under her hand. "Do. Not. Speak. To. Me. We are done here. You and I, we are done." With that, she walked out of the kitchen, her room door slamming shut a few seconds later.

"Oh my God, Lane, what did I do?" I said, still stunned. I had never hit anyone before, not with the intent to hurt them. "I hit her, Lane, I really hit her. I'm a horrible person."

Lane stepped in front of me, rubbing my arms. "You're okay, Abby. Whitney said some horrible things. I could hear them from the living room. You reacted on instinct and lashed out. It happens. And you apologized. That does not make you a horrible person. If you had enjoyed it and wanted to do it again, then you would be a horrible person."

I nodded, trying to take in his words. "I should give her some space. I know she won't want to talk to me anytime soon."

Lane nodded. "I think that's a great idea. Just give her a few days, and maybe you guys can talk then."

A few days. Except that in a few days I would be leaving everyone here behind. But if she wasn't real anyway, then should I even care? Or should I just let it be and deal with the consequences on my own?

Feeling the aftermath of the highs and lows of my emotions, I turned to Lane. "I think I need to go to bed. Go lay down or something."

"All right, let's go."

I took his hand and led him down the hall to my room, shutting the door softly. The bed was still rumpled from our earlier activities. I grabbed some pajamas out of a drawer and changed clothes quickly before jumping into bed. Lane took off his jeans and shirt, leaving his boxer briefs on before climbing in.

He wrapped his arms around me, pulling me into his body, his chest to my back. I rested my head on his arm, holding onto it for comfort. His other arm wrapped around my waist, keeping me secure. I loved the feeling of being secure in his arms. Lane made me feel safe. Something that I had sorely needed the last month and a half, ever since I had discovered the note that changed my life.

Taking in a deep breath, I savored Lane's smell before letting myself drift off into sleep.

Chapter Eleven

The next day was tense between me and Whitney. I only saw her a few times and one of those times she had a small duffel bag packed with some of her things. It saddened me to think she was going to such lengths to ignore and avoid me. All I really wanted was to talk to her. My time was running out and I didn't want to leave things on such a bad note between us.

Friday morning, I reached into my desk drawer and took out the note that I had written for Whitney. I read it again a couple times, making sure that everything I wanted to say was in there.

What I wanted to put in there was a giant list of all the amazing memories that we had made. Or how I had been there for her through her numerous breakups with her stupid boyfriends. I didn't want to leave like this. But there was nothing else I could do. She had made up her mind and wasn't giving me the chance to change it.

Sighing, I stood up and put the note back in the drawer. I would deal with that later. Right now, I had to get ready for tonight. I was meeting Lane for lunch in a few hours and Whitney was at work all day. She would probably be gone tonight too. I was sure she wasn't coming back to the apartment, not while she knew I was there.

I took my time getting ready, wanting to look my best for the last time I saw Lane. Tears kept running down my face, and after a while, I stopped trying to wipe them away. This was my goodbye to him, even if he didn't know it.

As if on cue, Lane knocked on the front door. I grabbed my purse and went to meet him. Opening the door, a sense of déjà vu hit me. I realized this reminded me of our first date. He came to pick me up and I remember being so nervous. And Whitney...Whitney had helped me so much that day. More tears threatened to fall as I stood there looking at him.

He noticed and moved in, hands cupping my face, giving me a gentle kiss. "Hey, it's going to be okay. She's going to come around. She can't stay mad forever."

I bit my lip and nodded, not wanting to try to speak in case I started weeping. I wasn't about to correct him and tell him my tears were for him and not for Whitney.

We left and went down to Lane's car and drove to a restaurant that had a laid-back vibe to it. With all the decorations adorning the walls, it was hard for me to unwind. It seemed that every clock I saw was blaring at me, forcing me to countdown in my head how much time I had left.

Ten hours

The buzzing of everyone around us was becoming too much. I couldn't focus on anything Lane was saying. What a horrible way to spend my last hours with him.

Nine hours

"Do you think we can go home?" I asked him. "I mean, back to my place? I'm not feeling well right now."

Lane's brow furrowed as he looked at me, concern all over his face. "Yeah, sure. Just let me get the bill and we can go."

I wiped my mouth off with my napkin and stood up. "Do you mind if I wait outside? I think the fresh air will help me out."

"Sure," Lane said slowly. "I'll be right there."

I got up and hurried outside. Letting out a breath I hadn't realized I was holding, I sucked in more air, hoping it would settle me down. *Calm yourself!* I thought. *You can't break down now.*

Looking up, I noticed that the sky was darkening. Clouds were moving in, matching my dark mood. I didn't want to see sunshine right now, so the storm coming in was perfect for how I was feeling at the moment.

The door behind me cracked open and Lane's arm wrapped around my shoulder while he bent down to kiss my temple. "Are you okay now?"

Nodding, I plastered a fake smile onto my face. "Yeah, a little better. You ready to go?"

"Yeah, let's get going."

We drove in silence, holding hands across the center console. I rubbed my thumb back and forth over the back of Lane's hand, taking the time to appreciate how firm and strong it felt. These hands have wiped my tears, held my own hands, and worshipped me as we lied in bed. They have protected me, and they have supported me. *What was I going to do without him?*

Reaching the apartment, we went upstairs, and I turned on a movie on the television. Sitting down, I cuddled into Lane's arms, savoring the feel. I never wanted to forget this feeling.

I jolted up, rubbing my eyes. What time was it? What happened? Thunder rumbled, and I realized that was what had woken me up. Outside, it was beginning to thunderstorm. Lane shifted under me, groaning as he opened his eyes.

"Did we fall asleep?" I asked.

Lane stretched, rubbing his face. "Yeah. Good thing I'd already seen that movie."

Seven hours

I had wasted the afternoon. Wasted it! Anger and resentment welled up inside of me. "This is not okay," I whispered.

Lane sat up, confusion on his face. "Abby, it's fine. We didn't miss anything. We're fine."

I shook my head back and forth, hiding my face in my hands. "We missed *everything*."

"Abby, you're not making sense."

Taking a shaky breath, I looked up at Lane. "I'm sorry. You're right. I think the nap just…disoriented me or something."

Lane smiled at me, rubbing my back. Telling me he would be right back, he stood up and went down the hall to my bedroom. I stood up and started pacing back and forth. What else did I need to get done before tonight? Whitney. But there was only a tiny chance that she would come home while I was there tonight, let alone come home at all.

Whatever. I had a note I was going to leave her. There was no need to get even more worked up over it. As she loved to point out lately, she's not real, so there's no point in being mad. I rolled my eyes at the thought.

Lane came back in and pulled me in for a hug, affectively breaking me out of my thoughts. "Are you sure you're okay? You've been acting a little...off today."

I nodded, hoping that my face looked normal. "I am. I just wish I hadn't fallen asleep. It just feels like it's messing up my day. Makes it harder to go to sleep at night if I take a nap during the daytime."

"I get that. Sometimes it messes me up too. Anyway, I got a call from Kent. He needs me back at the house to help him fix something. Are you going to be okay here by yourself?"

"Yeah, I'll be okay." I enveloped him in a hug, holding him tightly to me.

He kissed the top of my head, hugging me. "I love you, Abby."

I looked up at him, trying to memorize his face before he left. "I love you too, Lane. So much."

His gaze softened as he looked at me. He leaned down for a kiss that I deepened, enjoying the feel of him on me. Pulling back, he grinned at me. "I love that, too. Can't wait to do more of that with you later."

I tried to smile and managed to pull the corners of my lips up in a resemblance to one. "I can't wait either. Now, go help your brother. I'll see you later."

Lane gave me a smile that melted my heart as I watched him go. Then I heaved in a breath as the door shut behind him and I slid down the wall to the floor, sobs wrenching me as I cried my heart out. The pain I felt at him leaving was nothing that I had thought I would feel. I would never see him again. That was it. My last time talking to Lane, touching Lane, kissing Lane. It was done. Over. He was gone. That thought brought a fresh round of tears to my eyes and I slumped down, pressing my face into my hands.

I sat there for what seemed like forever. Eventually, my mind seemed to come back to me and I took a deep breath. Sitting up, I swiped my hair back from my face, straightening it out. Wiping my tears off, I stood up, dusting off as I steadied myself. I looked around the apartment, trying to memorize every detail.

Six hours

Walking down the hall, I entered Whitney's room. I knew I shouldn't have, but with her acting how she was, I just wanted to remember her as she used to be, as my best friend. I looked at the framed pictures she had hanging up on the walls and sitting on her desk. I was surprised to see that quite a few of them were of us. I had figured that she would have thrown away anything that reminded her of me.

I sat on her bed, holding a frame of the two of us. We had our arms around each other and were laughing at something one of us had said. It was taken about a year after she had moved in and we had become such close friends since. Tears escaped my eyes as I closed them tightly, wanting to savor the good memories and not those of the last few days.

Okay, I had to get out of here before I withered away from crying so much. I stood up, setting the picture back down before I left. Continuing to my own room, I went inside, shutting the door behind me. I took the note that had changed my life out of my bag and looked at it, smoothing it flat. Reading it again, I thought back to how this tiny thing had turned my life upside down. Was it a blessing or a curse? I still wasn't sure.

Five hours

Time was flying by. Like that saying, time flies when you're not looking forward to doing something. I was *really* not looking forward to this.

I went back to the living room and turned on the television, not paying any attention to what was on. I left it on some reality show while I sat there contemplating what was going to happen.

Four hours

It was going too fast. I started pacing the living room. I wasn't ready. I couldn't do this. This was insane, whose idea was this anyway? My idiotic idea, of course. No, I could always change my mind. I didn't have to do this. I could stay here with Lane forever. I could tell Whitney I had temporarily lost my mind and I was wrong and she was right. I could make this work.

But at what cost? Didn't I owe it to myself to figure out the truth?

Yes. Yes, I did owe myself the truth. I couldn't keep lying to myself about what was going on. I had to know.

Three hours

I could swear I was wearing a trail into the apartment floor. I couldn't stop myself walking from the kitchen to the living room, down the hallway and back again, only to start the cycle back over.

Two hours

Should I pack something? No, that was stupid. Why would I bring something with me? I was going to wake up, there was no logical way that I could bring something with me for that. I sighed, going into my room. Picking up a picture of Lane and myself, I could only stare at it, running a finger over Lane's half. I could feel the tears threatening to spill, the hotness pricking at my eyes. Drawing in a deep breath, I pushed them back, not wanting to be dragged into another cry-fest tonight.

One hour

What the hell? How was the time passing so quickly? I started pacing again, worrying about everything that could go wrong. The car might not show up. What if it didn't hit me hard enough and nothing happened? What if it hit me and I just died? I shuddered to think of that. There were so many *what if's* that I could feel myself backing out of the plan.

What if?

What if...

What

if?

This was destroying me. Do I or don't I? Yes or no? I hid my face in my hands and sat down on the couch. I had to stay strong. I had to do this. I was going on such a downhill spiral already, if I didn't do this, the hallucinations would just keep going and ruin me.

It was time.

Drawing a deep breath, I stood up and looked around, making sure everything was in its place. I walked to my room and got my note for Whitney and walked to her room with it. I brought it to my mouth, gave it a kiss, and laid it down on her bed, propped up on her pillows. I wanted to make sure that she would see it first thing. I just prayed that she came home before I finished my plan, so that she would have time to see my note and know how much I had come to love her as my best friend and how much I relied on her.

Going into my room, I changed my clothes, trying to get more comfortable. Pulling on jeans and a t-shirt, I grabbed a pair of shoes and sat down to tie them. Looking out the window, I saw that the rain was pouring down harder than it was earlier, so I grabbed a hoodie and pulled it on, shielding myself against the onslaught I was about to encounter.

Breathing deeply, I left the apartment, locking the door behind me. I ran down the stairs, not wanting to wait on the elevator, then I burst out of the front doors. The air was rushing in and out of me, giving me a bit of a high that I only just now realized that I needed.

The rain beat down, my hair clinging to my face and shoulders. I laughed, raising my face to the sky, relishing in the cleansing that I was experiencing. It was like all my sins were rinsing off me and I could turn a fresh face onto the next portion of my life. I turned to face the direction that The Den was in. That was where I needed to go. I could only hope that the rain didn't change anything for me.

Three blocks had gone by before I heard my name being yelled. Turning around, my stomach dropped as I saw Lane chasing me down the street, calling for me.

"What are you doing Lane?" I yelled over the rain.

He stopped right in front of me, breathing hard. "Me? What the hell, Abby? Whitney just called me, and she was all bent out of shape about some note that you left her saying you were leaving or something? What are you doing?"

My insides warmed a little at the thought that Whitney had gotten my note and had cared about what I said. I had to shake it off though; I couldn't let feelings get in the way of what I needed to do.

"It's fine, Lane. I'm doing what needs to be done."

Lane walked closer and put his hands on my arms, holding me in place. "What exactly are you planning, Abby?"

I shook my head, not looking at him. If I did, I would only start crying again. "Please, Lane, don't worry about me. Just go home."

"Go home? I can't leave you if I think you're going to do something stupid."

"It's not stupid! It's going to finish everything for me!"

Lane looked at me, incredulous, raindrops clinging to his eyelashes. "Finish everything? What exactly are you doing Abby? Tell me!"

I shook my head, tears pouring down now. I wiped at my face before I realized that the rain wasn't helping matters. My face was wet whether it was from the rain or from my tears. "You don't get it! My life is in ruins right now! I can't keep going on like this! I have to stop it!"

I tried to turn around to keep walking, but Lane grabbed my arm, yanking me back around to face him.

"Abby, stop! You are not going to do anything like what I think you're doing! What about Whitney? What about *me*?" The pain in his eyes caused a crack in my heart, pain pouring through it. "We were made for each other, Abby. You know that, and I know that! You can't just leave me like this! It's not fair to me!"

I covered my face with my hands. "I know it's not! I know, okay!" I looked at him. "It's not like I want to leave you. I don't. But I have to do this!"

"Do what?"

I didn't answer him right away. I just looked at him, getting in my last glimpses. "I have to finish the note. I have to wake up."

"And how are you planning to do that?"

I exhaled and wiped the hair back from my face. "I don't want to tell you, Lane. Please, just drop it."

"No," he said forcefully.

Anger surged through me. "No? You can't tell me what to do Lane."

"Maybe not, but I love you Abby. Doesn't that count for something?"

"Of course it does! But not with this!"

"You either love me or you don't! Which is it, Abby?"

More tears came out, flowing down my cheeks as I tried to keep my breathing even. "Of course I love you, damn it! But this isn't about you! It's about me!"

"No, it's about *us*! I matter here too, Abby. I matter too! Why didn't you try to talk to me about this?"

I huffed out a laugh, shaking my head. "I did! I told you and Whitney both what I was thinking, that I thought the note was real. What did you think would happen?"

Lane ran a hand through his hair. "I don't know! But not you stopping anything. What does that even mean?"

I couldn't answer him. I didn't want to see the disappointment on his face when I told him what I was planning to do. I couldn't let Lane down. He was my everything. Thunder crashed, causing me to jump a little, my heartbeat speeding up.

He stepped closer, wrapping his arms around my waist to hold me close. "Tell me," he whispered. "Please, don't shut me out."

I laid my head down on his shoulder for a minute, inhaling his scent, letting it stir up the memories that I loved. Lifting it, I looked him straight in the eyes. "The car."

I could see the moment when Lane understood what I meant. His forehead was scrunched up, confusion in his eyes. After a few seconds, it cleared up, horror replacing it. He opened his mouth to say something, but nothing came out. Backing up a few steps, he shook his head, rubbing a hand over his jaw like he could force himself to bring out the words he wanted.

I took the opportunity to take a few steps back, trying to head toward my goal. I didn't want to have this conversation. I didn't want to break Lane's heart like my own was broken. This was why I had left a note. This was why I had tried to sneak out.

"Don't leave me, Abby!"

I froze and realized I had turned around to start walking. I looked back, and Lane was reaching out to me, panic written on his face.

He ran to me and wrapped his arms around me, whispering frantically. "Don't leave me, please don't leave me. Abby, I love you, stay with me."

My heart broke some more, and I let out a sob, holding Lane tightly, wishing I could bring him with me. We stood there for a minute, both of us crying, before I gently pushed Lane away from me.

I put a hand on his cheek, rubbing my thumb back and forth. "I love you, Lane. So much. But I have to. I have to do this."

"No. No. Stay with me. Here. Stay with me. Please, Abby." Lane's face crumpled.

"I'd be living a lie, Lane. I can't do that." I took a few steps back, trying to fortify my heart.

"You would be here with me. Isn't that enough?"

And the worst part was, it was enough. *Almost.* God, it was almost enough for me. Why couldn't it just be enough? The rain and my tears were mixing even more, making it difficult for me to see as I cried even harder.

"Lane, God, I wish it was! But I can't forget about it, because I'll always be living with the fear of another hallucination! Another freak out! Another scary, realistic dream! I can't live like that. I wish I could just stay here with you and be happy and forget that any of this had ever happened!"

He stepped toward me and grabbed my hand, holding it tightly in both of his. "Then do it, Abby! Stay with me. Stay *for* me! Can't you do that? Aren't I enough for you?"

A sharp pain jabbed at my chest. If I told the truth, I would hurt him. If I lied, I would hurt myself. This was an impossible decision. It was made even more impossible by the fact that I didn't know what I was doing, not really. I could be completely wrong about the car theory and just be killing myself. But it was the small voice in me asking *what if?* that was keeping me going.

I slowly loosened my hand, pulling away from him. "You are, Lane. You are enough." I took a deep breath and took a step back. "You are enough if I could be absolutely certain that this was all real." I gestured at everything around us. "If I knew that, yes, I could stay and be happy."

Lane seemed stunned silent by my confession. "*If* you could be certain? *If* you thought this was real, that I'm real?" He dropped his gaze, and I felt a pang of guilt that he couldn't reach my eyes.

"I'm so sorry, Lane. I do love you. You don't even know how much I love you. I've never felt this way about anyone. I feel completed in a way that I never have before. You've given me so much. I just…I just need to do this."

Before I could think anymore, I turned away from him and started walking. Walking away from my heart, away from my other half, my soulmate. The crushing sensation I was feeling in my chest was like nothing I had felt before. Was this what a broken heart felt like? Was I just broken now?

I didn't hear Lane pursuing me, which made me feel worse. Even though I wasn't going to change my mind, I wanted him to come after me. I wanted him to try to stop me, to want me to stop what I was planning. Did he not care anymore? Had I broken him, too?

Taking a shaky breath, I continued another block until I reached my destination. The Den was across the street, and I could see a few groups of people waiting around outside, some people smoking and some on the phone with their friends. It was such a normal scene that it took my breath away. That used to be me. I used to come here with my friends, with Whitney, and not know that anything could be different.

I glanced around, trying to pinpoint where the red car was going to be coming from. The rain was still falling, obscuring my view. I could feel the anxiety setting in, my pulse racing. The doubts were creeping in, and I couldn't help but feel like what I was doing was wrong.

I turned in a circle, starting to wonder what the hell I was doing here. *Why am I doing this?* I asked myself. *Just because of some stupid note?* I was an idiot. Of course, I should stay with Lane.

But *what if?*

Groaning, I covered my face with my hands and stomped my foot. I hated being so wishy-washy. I just needed to know what the truth was!

A tingling awareness started pricking at the back of my neck, like that feeling when you just know that someone is staring at you. It was coming. It was almost time. I headed to the corner to wait, but my arm was yanked back as someone grabbed it.

Turning to yell, I stopped when I saw Lane standing there holding my wrist with both hands. His eyes were rimmed red and his nose was slightly colored. More tears fell from my eyes as I saw how much I was hurting him. It was the last thing that I wanted to do.

"I have to go, Lane."

"No, you don't. Stay with me. Stay."

I shook my head, my hood falling down and the rain completely soaking me, my hair sticking to my face. "I can't. I have to do this."

I tugged my wrist from his hands and took a few steps backward, toward the road. Looking past Lane, I could see a shine of red coming in our direction. I had maybe a minute more before I had to go.

I turned and walked away from Lane, my heart breaking some more at leaving him. I hated this. I hated that I was here, that I was questioning everything for something that I wasn't even sure was real.

Lane followed me, hands running through his hair. I could tell that he was about to do something drastic, like pick me up and carry me off himself if I didn't go with him willingly. The car was getting closer and it seemed like time was slowing down, letting me see everything in slow motion with clarity.

Taking a deep breath, I looked around at everything one more time, letting the memories of my life wash over me. They flowed through me and I felt lighter when I turned back to Lane. I stepped to him and wrapped him in my arms as tightly as I could. He hugged me back, crushing me, whispering words of love.

I leaned back and looked him in the eyes. "I love you, Lane. Never forget that." I kissed him, hoping that he could feel all my unspoken words and wishes in that one kiss.

The despair in his eyes when I broke apart from him would haunt me forever, no matter what happened to me. I took a step away from him and he grabbed my hand again, pleading with me to stay.

Not being able to bear the pain anymore, I yanked my hand away from his and turned away, running toward the street.

"Abby, no! Don't do this!"

I shut my ears against his pleas and kept moving. Turning to look, I saw the red car coming to meet me in the street, as if we were meeting for one final dance.

The car rushed around the corner, and just like that, time went back to its normal pace.

And I jumped.

Chapter Twelve

The pain.

That was the first thing that my body sensed.

Then everything happened at once.

People shouting.

Tires squealing.

Glass flying.

The agony was everywhere. It was like fire flowing over my skin, piercing through it in different spots. Fire stabbed into my thigh, lighting me up from the inside. It went into my shoulder, and I could feel it coursing through from the front to the back.

The agonizing fire grazed my ribs, making me wish for oblivion.

The car hit me, forcing me up onto its windshield. I screamed, trying to shield my face with my hands, but I was moving too fast to be able to do anything. The glass cracked and then collapsed around me. The momentum of the hit rolled me back down to the street, but the car couldn't stop in time from hitting me again as I connected to the pavement, the left side of my head bouncing on the street, ripping another scream from me.

And then blessed darkness.

I opened my eyes, but the world was too blurry to make anything out. Voices were shouting all around me and hands were touching me, setting the fire ablaze even more. I groaned, trying to move away from their hands but I was immobile. My arms and legs were strapped down, and I couldn't move my head.

"Abby, Abby, can you hear me?" Frantic shouting sounded to my right. I rolled my eyes in that direction and could barely make out Lane through the blur.

"Sir, you need to move back," an authoritative voice said.

"I'm not leaving her. Abby, I'm not leaving you! You're going to be okay!" His voice was getting fainter as he was moved away from where I was lying.

Glass was being pulled out of me, the sharp pains of it sliding through my skin enough to make a black haze overcome me.

The next time I opened my eyes I was looking at the ceiling of a van, and I could hear beeping all around me and people talking.

"...lost about two liters of blood..."

"Glass everywhere..."

"Get that I.V. going!"

"What the hell was she thinking?"

"Hey, she's awake. Ma'am, can you..."

I closed my eyes and welcomed the darkness.

Voices started to come back, but my vision stayed black. I couldn't tell if I even had my eyes open or not. Why wouldn't the pain stop? I thought this was my answer to everything. I ruined it all. I was so stupid.

"Quick, get the crash cart!"

"She's lost too much..."

What? No, I couldn't die now. Not when I could see that I was wrong about everything.

"No, Abigail, don't you quit on me now!"

No, no, I didn't want to quit. Don't let me quit.

I managed to open my eyes halfway. Doctors were standing over me, frantic and covered in blood. *My blood.* One saw me and leaned down over me, speaking words of encouragement.

Or at least I thought she was. I couldn't hear her anymore. I gave her a faint smile to show her that everything was fine. It didn't hurt anymore. They had done a fantastic job of fixing me. I just wanted to go home now. Go home and go to sleep. Just a short nap. I was so tired.

Why was the doctor crying? Tears filled her eyes as she looked at me, but I smiled again, trying to show her that I was okay.

It was time to sleep now.

Chapter Thirteen

The darkness seemed to be getting lighter. I tried looking around, but it was all black. How did I get out of here? I swallowed, made difficult by my dry and swollen tongue. Groaning, I moved my tongue around, trying to get some saliva moving.

There was a constant beeping sound to my right. *Heart monitor*, my instinct told me. What? Where was I?

A door opened, and footsteps walked toward me, the sound of paper rustling with it. I could hear the person sigh and mutter, "Still no change, huh, Abigail?"

Then, "Wait, what's this?" More paper moved around and the person gasped. "Abigail, can you hear me?"

My eyes were opened and a light shone in them, back and forth. I blinked a few times, trying to get rid of the spots in my vision.

Soon I was able to see a young woman standing in front of me, grinning. "This is incredible! I'll be right back!"

I couldn't move my head to nod, nor open my mouth to respond. The panic I felt at those restrictions caused me to breathe faster, and I shifted my eyes back and forth, trying to figure out where I was.

It was a small room and I seemed to be the only person in it. The walls were a light shade of green with generic landscape pictures hanging on the walls. Based on the heart monitor I could still hear, I figured there was medical equipment close by me that I couldn't see, since I wasn't able to move. There was a small, round table with two chairs in the corner across from me and a window to my left with white curtains that were pulled back to let the sunshine in. The door to the room was to my right and suddenly, the woman and two other people entered back in.

The two new people, who I assumed to be doctors, came over to me and started examining me, testing my eyes' reflexes and checking the printouts from the machines I was hooked up to.

"Abigail, can you hear me?" asked one of the doctors.

I tried to open my mouth to answer, but it was so dry that nothing came out. Panic flared, and my eyes widened. The doctor saw my distress and shushed me, calming me down.

"Abigail, it's okay. I know it must be hard for you to comprehend what's going on right now and you're probably in pain and thirsty. First, we need to do some tests on you to get a better idea of what's going on."

I nodded. Or at least I thought I did, but I'm not sure my head actually moved. I felt weighted down, like a heavy blanket was on top of me, suffocating me. *Maybe that's why I can't move*, I thought to myself.

Soon enough, the doctors came back and wheeled me out of the room. The afternoon flew by in a series of tests and machines. I noticed that the whole time, other nurses and doctors would poke their heads into the room and watch me, tears in their eyes and happy smiles on their faces.

I fell asleep at some point, sinking into oblivion, dreaming of nothing. When I next opened my eyes, the young woman I first saw was sitting in the chair at the round table, writing on a clipboard. I must have made a noise, because she looked up suddenly at me, her face breaking out into a smile.

"You're awake! Great! You have some visitors if you're up for it."

I slowly nodded my head up and down, pleased to find out that I could move it now.

She left, and I let out a breath. Since I could move my head a little, I decided to test out the rest of my body. I concentrated on my hands first and moved them back and forth a little bit. My feet had the same results. I was able to move them left and right. My whole arms and legs were a different story. When I tried to bend them, even a little bit, I discovered that I couldn't move them. That heavy blanket sensation I had felt before came back, keeping me from moving as much as I wanted to.

The effort exhausted me. I had just woken up and I was already on the verge of another nap. I had just closed my eyes and started to doze when I heard the door open again. Opening my eyes was such a strain that I decided to keep them closed instead.

"Oh my God, Ed." I heard the woman come closer. "Abigail, sweetie, can you hear me? It's mommy. Wake up, baby, please wake up for me." She sounded close to tears.

I took a deep breath and struggled against the fatigue I was feeling and opened my eyes. The woman standing over me gasped, covering her mouth with her hands, tears spilling over.

"Mom," I whispered, barely able to hear the word.

She choked out a laugh, quiet whimpers turning into loud cries as she took my hand and bent down to give it a kiss. I glanced over at the man, my eyes filling with tears. "Dad," I said, trying to smile.

He came around to my other side and took hold of my hand, eyes misty. The nurse stood off in the corner, her hand covering her mouth as she tried to hold in her own tears at our reunion.

I shifted my eyes back and forth between them, trying to figure out what was going on. "What..." I murmured, not able to finish the sentence. *What was going on? Where was I?* I had so many questions about what had happened, and I couldn't ask them.

"Sweetie, do you remember anything that happened?" My mom bent down and brushed the hair off my forehead.

I shook my head. There was nothing there. Then I got a flash of a memory. A car. Screaming. Pain.

"Car," I said, wincing at my dry throat.

Dad saw my expression and asked the nurse for a glass of water for me. She nodded quickly and left the room. He turned back to me and gave me a small smile, squeezing my hand in encouragement.

"Abigail, you were in a car accident. You were hit by a car one night and suffered a lot of different injuries," my mom said. "The worst one was your head. You hit it extremely hard when you fell, and you were brought in unconscious. It's been…it's been five years, Abigail. You've been unconscious and in a coma for five years."

I could only stare at her. That was impossible. I was in an accident the night before. It was only last night I did that, wasn't it?

"No," I said, trying to shake my head. "No."

Mom sniffed, wiping her eyes and cheeks. "Yes, sweetie, it was five years ago. I'm so sorry this happened to you, but I'm so happy that you're awake now. You were in the hospital while you were healing from your broken bones and other things, but we moved you to a long-term care facility that could monitor you a little more privately than a hospital could."

"Whitney?" I asked, hoping they would understand what I meant.

Mom and Dad looked at each other, confusion on their faces. Dad looked down at me and said, "I'm sorry, honey, we don't know anyone named Whitney. No one with that name came by to see you."

My heart sank, and my stomach rolled at that information. I could feel bile rising up the back of my throat and I started coughing on it, trying to keep it down. I moved my head to the side and started wheezing, unable to get enough air in my lungs.

Whitney wasn't real. *Lane.* Tears came pouring out as I started bawling, feeling all the sadness and pain at the fact that they were gone. They were just gone. And I had never made up with Whitney. And Lane was just *gone.* They both were. How did I move on from this?

The nurse came back in with a glass of water and quickly came over to my bed, raising the back of it so I was sitting more upright. "Okay, okay, here we go. Can you take a small drink of water, Abigail? Can you do that for me? Maybe it'll help you calm down." She raised the straw in the glass to my mouth and I took a sip, letting it quench my thirst.

Mom moved back over to my side, fear in her eyes at my breakdown. "Is Whitney a friend of yours? Do you want us to call her?"

I shook my head, unable to meet her eyes. How did I tell her Whitney was a friend that I had made up while I *dreamed up* the past five years? I knew I had told myself that I believed the note I had received was real, but it never prepared me for the pain of realizing what would happen once I woke up and my best friends were gone. That they were never there in the first place.

The nurse looked over my charts again and smiled at me. "Abigail, the doctor who's been treating you, Dr. Cole, is on his way, okay? He should be here shortly. He was actually on vacation, but when we called him to say that you had woken up, he said he was coming right in."

I nodded, not caring at all if some doctor were coming in or not. At this point I was regretting my decision to jump in front of that car. I wanted to go back. I wanted to go back to my dream and have Whitney and Lane with me. I was so stupid. I didn't know what I had until it was gone. And I was never getting it back.

Mom and Dad walked over to the nurse in the corner, speaking in hushed tones with her. Occasionally, they would glance over at me and the nurse would shake her head at something one of them would say. I didn't even try to be curious. Obviously, they were talking about me.

I closed my eyes, weariness taking over me. Blackness consumed me, and I was gone. I was dreaming about Lane. We were out on a date somewhere, but I didn't look around me. All I could focus on was Lane. I wanted to drink him in and savor the moment of just being with him again. Finally, he spoke to me and I smiled.

"Abigail? Can you hear me?"

I frowned, groaning. I did not want to wake up, not when I was dreaming about Lane.

"Abigail?"

That voice.

I opened my eyes and saw I was facing the window. The sun had shifted over so not as much light was coming in. I turned my head and froze.

Lane.

I gasped, my eyes filling with tears again. This wasn't real. This wasn't happening. I was still dreaming, wasn't I?

He smiled at me and took my hand. "Abigail, I'm Dr. Cole. I can't begin to tell you how excited I am to see you awake. It's been a long five years for all of us here, but I know especially for your parents."

I looked behind him to see Mom and Dad watching us, beaming.

"How are you here?" I whispered.

His brow furrowed, *just like it always did when he was concerned about me*, and he patted my hand. "Well, I'm your doctor. Yours is an interesting and rare case and we've been doing a lot of things to try to bring you out of your coma."

He stepped back so Mom and Dad could come in closer. "If you two wouldn't mind, I'm going to go over Abigail's charts and then I'll come back and we can talk." He turned to leave.

"Lane," I said, not wanting him to leave.

He turned around in surprise, looking at me. "How did you know my name?" He looked at Mom and Dad, but they both shook their heads.

"We haven't said anything," Mom said.

Dr. Cole nodded, a pensive look on his face, and he looked at me again. "I'll be back soon so we can talk."

I nodded, not ready to watch him leave. I kept my eyes on the door long after he walked through it.

Mom turned to me. "How did you know his name?"

Keeping my eyes on the door, I said, "Because he was there in my dream. Because I'm in love with him."

I heard her sharp intake of breath and knew she was looking at Dad, wondering what to do. He stepped up and patted my shoulder. "Let's just see what he has to say when he comes back."

It took thirty more minutes before Lane, *Dr. Cole, his name is Dr. Cole,* came back to see us. He gestured for my parents to sit at the table while he stood at the foot of my bed so he was able to see all of us at the same time.

"So, Ed and Sherry, I know you already know this, so I'm going to catch Abigail up on what's been going on." They nodded and he turned to me. "Abigail, your parents told you that you've been in a coma, correct?"

I nodded.

"Good. It was a pretty severe one. The injuries you sustained in your accident should have done worse than that. You're lucky to be alive. You were moved here after you were finished healing at the hospital. It's more private than a hospital, plus the care is more personalized. I was the one who took your case. It's been a long five years, Abigail. Nothing we were doing to stimulate you to wake up was working. Your scans were all coming back clear, showing us that there was still brain activity. Your body had just decided to shut down and retreat into itself."

This was a lot to take in. Hearing the gritty details about something that I couldn't even remember was weird.

Dr. Cole continued. "There was a technology that we came across called DreamScape that we thought we would take a gamble on. It's an extremely new procedure and is still in the testing phase. We knew you were having dreams in your coma based on scans we were doing. This new technology allowed us to implant suggestions into your dream."

The blood left my face and dizziness rushed over me. I knew exactly what they were talking about.

"The note," I said softly.

Dr. Cole nodded. "I'm guessing you know what we're talking about then? We didn't know how it would present itself to you in your dream. We didn't even know if it would work. Like I said, this was still experimental and new. We had to hook you up to a machine and a computer and one of the DreamScape techs wrote in a code that would appear to you in a natural state in your dream. Can you tell us about it?"

I nodded and tried to lift myself up straighter. The heavy blanket feeling was receding, and I was feeling more in control of my body. I could tell that I was extremely weak though and I was far too thin.

"It was a note. I had this whole life. I remembered everything, I had no idea none of it was real. I had a job, a roommate, a boyfriend." At this, I couldn't help but look at Dr. Cole, who curiously enough blushed and looked away. "I was an editor at a publishing company and the note came in one of my manuscripts. It scared the living daylights out of me. Nobody could see it except for me and—" Again, I paused, looking at Dr. Cole. He nodded at me to continue.

"It said I had been in a coma for five years and that I needed to wake up. It was insane. I started hallucinating, hearing voices. I hated it. Every moment of it. I felt like I was going crazy." Tears were slipping down my cheeks, and when I looked at my parents, I saw that they were crying too.

Mom rushed out of her seat and gathered me in a hug, crying. "I'm so sorry, sweetie. I'm so sorry this happened to you." She rocked me back and forth.

Dad cleared his throat and wiped his eyes dry. "So, what's the next step, Doctor? What do we do now?"

"Well, now we just get Abigail into rehab. She needs to relearn how to walk, how to sit, basically build up her muscles that she hasn't been using for five years. Plus, we're going to have talks about her time in her coma, see what all she remembers from before the accident and what her dreams were like while she was under. She may want to talk to a professional, a psychiatrist, to help her deal with coming back to the real world."

My parents nodded, as if I hadn't just had a life altering experience. I couldn't help but let tears fall down my cheeks as I tried to process the events of the last day.

Dr. Cole was the first to notice and cleared his throat, looking uncomfortable. Dad came over to join Mom in comforting me, trying to calm me down.

That only made me cry harder. I didn't know what else to do. How was I supposed to accept all of this? Was this supposed to be okay?

"Well, I think Abigail has had enough to deal with today. How about we give her some room, so she can rest if she wants to?" Dr. Cole suggested.

Mom and Dad nodded, and each gave me a kiss before heading out the door together. Dr. Cole lingered behind, fidgeting with his clipboard and papers.

"Maybe we could have a talk later? Just to fill you in on some more gaps?" he asked, sounding nervous.

I nodded. "Yes, I'd like that."

He gave a perfunctory nod and then left the room. I was left there in my bed, reeling from the day's information and events.

Lying back, I took a deep breath, hoping to steady myself. I had done it. I had beaten the coma and left it. Now I just needed to get my emotions in order. And figure out how the hell Lane was here. As a doctor. Did that mean that Whitney could be here too? Maybe I had been imagining people I already knew, and that's why they were in my dreams.

I must have fallen asleep, because the next thing I knew, a nurse was coming in with a tray of food, raising my bed so I could be sitting up.

Groaning, I pushed myself up straighter. The food looked...bland, at best. Applesauce, a slice of toast, and chicken noodle soup. I tried the soup first, only to find that it had no flavor. No seasoning or anything. I guessed it was straight from the can. Gross. I pushed it aside so I could eat the applesauce and toast. That part wasn't too bad at least.

I rang for the nurse after I was finished. My catheter had been removed earlier and I was hoping to get to the bathroom soon. The nurse came in and maneuvered me so I was sitting up. This was a lot harder than I thought it would be. I had broken out into a sweat and was shaking from the effort. Who knew just sitting up would be so hard? I guess Dr. Cole was right about needing a lot of physical therapy. How was I supposed to do anything for myself at this point?

The nurse helped me into a wheelchair and pushed me to the bathroom, helping me again as I sat down on the toilet. After I was finished, she wheeled me to the sink to wash my hands and then back to bed. By the time I was lying down again, I was sticky with sweat and breathing harshly. My legs were shaky and felt rubbery and my stomach muscles ached like I had just done a bunch of sit-ups. This was impossible. How would I recover from this?

The nurse smiled at me and patted me down with a towel. "This will get easier, trust me," she said. "The sooner you get back to using your muscles, the easier it will be."

I barely contained my eye roll, and instead went for a smile. "Thanks. I'll try to remember that." I already knew I was going to be tortured by my physical therapist.

The nurse left me alone and I drew the blankets up, thankful for the slight comfort they gave me. It was going to be an adjustment going from the world I knew to this one that was real.

At that moment, Dr. Cole came in the room, hesitating for a second when he saw me watching him. He walked over to a chair and brought it to my bedside and sat down. He sighed, running his hand through his hair, making my heart ache with the familiarity of the gesture. I couldn't keep from staring at it as it moved, hair whipping back into place as his hand moved through it.

"So, you have questions I presume," he said.

"A ton actually," I said, wishing he would just explain everything.

Dr. Cole sat there watching me for a minute before sighing and looking away. "You saw me, didn't you?" he asked as if he was sure of the answer.

I couldn't speak, astounded that he could tell what I was thinking. He knew?

Dr. Cole looked back up at me, waiting for an answer. I could only nod, wishing for words to form so I could ask him what was going on. He opened his mouth as if to answer, and then closed it again.

"Please just tell me what's going on," I pleaded. "I'm so confused. I thought I had lost everything when I woke up, but here you are."

"It's a long story," he started, "but I'll try to start at the beginning, so you'll know everything."

I nodded my agreement. This was what I wanted, to know everything.

"So," Dr. Cole started, "my name is Lane Cole." He stopped at my sharp inhale and held up his hand. "Please, let me just explain. You came in five years ago, recovering from your car accident and in a coma. We had tried everything, *everything* we could think of, to get you to wake up. Nothing was working. Your parents were losing hope of you ever waking up, but I didn't want you to become just another person in the system here.

"I spent most of my days in here with you, watching you and talking to you, hoping something would trigger you to wake up. That turned into me coming in on my breaks, eating or reading. I started reading to you out loud. I wasn't sure if you could hear anything in your coma, but I figured it couldn't hurt to try it. I didn't really know you, only things from what your parents said as I spoke to them about you. But I came to care about you in my own way."

His face turned red as he spoke, as if he was embarrassed to be divulging these secrets.

"So, I started to do more research on your case. I wanted to try to find similar cases, thinking maybe they would help me. In doing so, I came across DreamScape and their new technology that could be used for coma patients. It was a completely new thing, and it had only been used a couple of other times. At this point, I thought it couldn't hurt to try it. So, I talked to your parents about it, explained that it wasn't a sure thing, and they agreed to it.

"So they came out, we hooked you up to their machines and sent the note. I had asked the tech to add in some coding that would put in a copy of myself in your dream. It was something I didn't tell your parents about, but I had come to care for you and wanted to try anything to help you. We didn't know if it would work, of course. It was an extremely long shot, for both myself and the note we had sent you. DreamScape is still an up-and-coming company, but they are cutting edge technology, which is why I recommended them to your parents. They were desperate for you to wake up."

My head was whirling with all the information he was telling me. "You were there. You looked exactly the same as you do here. So you had no idea if it had worked or not? Or that you were there with me?"

Dr. Cole shook his head. "No, we didn't know if it would work. DreamScape is working on this now, to see if they can figure out a way to know if something that they send out is received in the minds of the patients. You are an amazing success case for them. I'm sure many others will be wanting to use them for their own families and patients now."

I just nodded, speechless.

He looked at me, hesitant. "So…can you tell me about it? You said I was there with you? What happened?"

I blushed, thinking of how we spent some of our last moments together. Dr. Cole noticed my red face and smiled a little bit, seeming amused.

"I, uh, well we met outside of a bar. You saved me actually," I stammered. "Your name was Lane Coleman. We started dating soon after that."

Dr. Cole really looked amused now, a twinkle in his eyes. "Did we now?"

I took a deep breath. "Yeah, we did. We dated and eventually I told you about the note. At that point, nobody else could see it. It just appeared to them as a normal piece of paper, just one page in a manuscript I was reading at the time. But to me, there was a section in there that was the note." I looked over at him. "But you could see it. How is that possible?"

Dr. Cole took a deep breath, rubbing his chin, mulling it over. "My thinking is that because the tech from DreamScape put in the coding for the note and for me at the same time, I was able to see the note. Nobody else could see it at all?"

I shook my head no.

"Well, I hope I was able to bring you some comfort while I was there."

"You did," I said. "You were my rock in there. I couldn't have done as much as I had without you there. I don't know what I would do without you."

Dr. Cole blushed and looked down. "Like I said, I came to care about you. Maybe my dream copy was the same way."

It was my turn to blush now. "Yeah, yeah you did. We loved each other."

He looked up sharply at that. "Really?"

"Yeah," I whispered. "And I don't know how to separate this real you from the you that I know."

Dr. Cole put a hand on top of mine. "I don't want you upset. I want you to take this time to recover and focus on you."

I searched his eyes, not sure what I would find there. I felt like my heart was breaking again. I hadn't realized until then that when I first saw him after waking that my hopes had gotten up, that maybe we could be together again. But it seemed that he didn't want me. He was just my doctor and that was it.

"Focus on me. Right. I'll do that," I said as I moved my hand away from his.

He grabbed it back and held on tighter. "I didn't mean it like that. You said you knew me in your dream. But I may not be the same person. I only know you as my patient. You might not be the same as I thought you were either." He paused, hesitating. "I want to get to know you, the real you. If that's okay with you. I won't be able to be your doctor anymore if I do though. It would be the whole conflict of interest thing, you know."

I felt my face glowing, the blood rushing to my cheeks. "You really want that? Even though you only know me as the girl who's been sleeping for five years?"

Dr. Cole nodded, face flushing. "Like I said, I came to care for you as I spent time with you here. It sounds absurd, I know. But I'm happy to hear that I was able to give you comfort in your dreams as you were dealing with trying to wake up."

"You had my back the whole time in there," I said. "I couldn't have done it without you."

Dr. Cole looked down at our entwined hands, and I noticed that I was absentmindedly rubbing his hand with my thumb. I stopped, blushing, thinking I was overstepping my bounds. He squeezed my hand, silently reassuring me that it was okay.

Epilogue

It took approximately an eternity for me to learn how to walk and be functional again. According to my parents, it was really only fourteen months, three weeks, and four days. *Only.* Yeah, okay. They weren't the ones crying at the ends of most days, screaming at their physical trainer to *just stop.* I threw a lot of things in those days. Whatever I could get my hands on, I threw it at my trainer. She didn't take it personally, thank goodness. She was used to being yelled at by most of her patients.

Of course, I was her only long-term coma patient that she had ever had. She wasn't sure what to expect of me, and honestly didn't expect me to recover one hundred percent anyway. After hearing that, I applied my whole being to exceeding her expectations. I wanted to prove to her, to everyone, that I could recover. That I was strong enough – stubborn enough, according to my parents – to overcome the mountains that rose up in front of me.

Dr. Cole – Lane – was there every step of the way. I had switched doctors so that we could explore what there was between us. I couldn't bring myself to stop loving him, even though he wasn't the same person that I had come to know and care about.

We didn't tell anyone about what we were doing at first. Then, one day, my mom came in during the day while he was visiting me on his lunch break. I was eating my own lunch, happy to have graduated to some more solid foods, and we were laughing about some story. Lane had his hand on mine and our fingers had slipped around each other's, binding us together.

I don't know how long she was standing there, but I looked up and saw Mom in the doorway, watching us. Her face was blank, and I couldn't tell what she was thinking. I almost pulled my hand away from Lane's, but then decided against it. There was nothing wrong with what I was doing.

Turned out that it didn't matter. Mom told me after Lane had left that she was happy for us. She could tell that there was something between us from the start. I confided in her all that had happened, from discovering Lane in my dreams to us talking about what we wanted with each other now. I explained that this was why he wasn't my doctor anymore, since it wouldn't be right, ethically.

This couldn't have gone better for me. I was recovering, my parents were okay with me being with Lane, and just the fact that there was a Lane for me to be with was what kept my spirits up.

The only black spot in me waking up was that there was no Whitney. I had a long talk with my parents about her, but they didn't know any of my friends by that name, nor anyone from my part-time job that I had held. It was devastating to know that she was gone forever, and I cried for days after being told the news. She had been the best friend that I had ever had, and even though she had only existed in my dream world, I still loved her and cherished the memory of her that I kept with me.

I was finally released to go home, with the promise of continuing to go in and keep up with my physical therapy. I could do most things, but I knew I still had a long road to go before I was back to my original self.

The day I came home, I didn't expect much. I was looking forward to a home cooked meal instead of hospital food. We got to the house and my jaw dropped. There were a ton of people inside waiting for me. People who were friends of my parents and people who I had known once upon a time and needed help to remember their names.

I went in and sat down on the couch, feeling a little overwhelmed. I wasn't sure whose idea this was, but I was feeling a little upset that I couldn't just sit down to a meal and then go to bed. I leaned my head back, ready to get this day over with already. I had been so excited and now I was too annoyed to enjoy myself.

I felt the couch dip down as someone sat beside me. Normally, I would have looked to see who it was, but I wasn't feeling too courteous at the moment.

"Are you okay?" I heard.

I jerked my head to the side and saw Lane sitting there. I gave him a small smile. He was just what I needed right now. "No, I'm kind of over this. I wasn't expecting anyone to be here when we got home. But the whole town is here, it looks like."

Lane smiled and grabbed my hand, pulling me in close to him. I tucked myself in, enjoying the sensation again.

He leaned in close, his breath stirring my hair. "Do you want to get out of here?"

I drew back, looking up at him and smiled. "You have no idea."

He stood up, drawing me up with him. He held my hand as we walked through the crowd to the back door. Opening it, he led me outside. The backyard was empty, everyone deciding to stay inside for the party.

I felt a weight lift off my shoulders that I hadn't even known was there. This was what I needed. Peace and quiet. I sighed, laying my head down on Lane's shoulder, relishing in the strength that he gave me. That he still gave me after all this time. We had become so close since I had woken up, it still surprised me sometimes. It was beyond what I had known of him in my dream world, but I loved it. I loved him.

Lane brought his arm around me and hugged me in closer. Breathing in his scent calmed me down and I rested against him, content.

"Are you okay?" he asked.

"Sort of. I'm overwhelmed by this homecoming. I didn't really want it, but I know that my parents are over the moon right now. So I can't really be mad about it. But I just want to go lie down and relax right now."

Lane kissed the top of my head and steered me to the porch swing that my Dad had installed while I was in high school. He sat me down and asked if I wanted a drink.

After he left, I laid my head back and closed my eyes. What a turn my life had taken. I wasn't sure where to go from here. Did I go back to college or stay home and get a job? What did I want to do with my life? I sighed and rubbed my eyes.

When I opened them, Lane was in front of me, kneeling so we were eye to eye. I smiled and leaned forward, giving him a kiss. I felt him kiss me back, making me fall under his spell even more.

When he broke the kiss, I groaned at the loss of contact. "No, I wasn't ready to be done," I pouted.

Lane grinned at me. "I'm not ready to be done either, Abigail. I love you so much. You have been through so much and I want to be there for you for everything. You are such a strong woman and you amaze me every day. You are my other half, my soulmate. Will you do me the honor of becoming my wife?"

He brought out a small, velvety black box and opened it, showing a white gold ring with a solitaire square cut diamond and smaller square cut diamonds surrounding it on the band. It was absolutely breathtaking.

I gasped, tears filling my eyes. I brought my hand to my mouth, trying to contain my breathing. "Oh my gosh, Lane, really? Of course, I'll marry you!"

Lane grinned, the tension leaving his shoulders. He brought my hand to his and slid the ring on and then kissed it after it was in place. I leaned forward, grabbing him close in a hug, holding him tightly to me.

Clapping erupted around us, and I looked up to notice that everyone had gravitated outside to watch Lane's proposal. Blood rushed to my face and I ducked my head down to hide it in Lane's shoulders, before starting to cry.

Lane rubbed my back to comfort me, but in the end, everyone was asked to leave the party so I could lie down and rest without feeling pressured to talk to all of our visitors.

Lane came up to my room with me and we laid down together, my head on his chest and his arm around my back. It was this position that I had found comforted me in my dream world and it brought me the same comfort now. It was made better by the knowledge that this wouldn't end.

This was real.

This was my life.

I couldn't wait to start it.

Acknowledgements

I would like to first off thank my husband, Gary, for being so patient with me while I wrote this book. I couldn't have done it without you!

To my parents, thank you for your support and encouragement as I wrote this.

To all my beta readers and Breanna, I couldn't have done this without your help. You guys helped me write a better book.

To all my readers. Thank you for taking this journey with me. I hope you enjoy reading it as much as I enjoyed writing it!